DEAD FOR DANGER

When a young Dublin woman is mugged and afterwards stabbed, the police look in vain for the attacker. But 49 Organ Place, the seedy apartment house where she lived, holds the secret which links her fate with that of a desperate and hunted man ... Detective Inspector Moss Coen is baffled by the discovery of another body. But when all the tenants suffer a final, devastating and deadly attack, the Inspector must go all out to find a merciless killer.

Books by Lorette Foley
in the Linford Mystery Library:

MURDER IN BURGOS
BURY BY NIGHT

LORETTE FOLEY

DEAD FOR DANGER

Complete and Unabridged

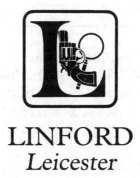

LINFORD
Leicester

·   British Library CIP Data

Foley, Lorette
    Dead for danger.—Large print ed.—
Linford mystery library
    1. Murder—Investigation—Ireland—Dublin
—Fiction 2. Detective and mystery stories
    3. Large type books
    I. Title
    823.9'14 [F]

ISBN 978–1–84617–791–0

Published by
F. A. Thorpe (Publishing)
Anstey, Leicestershire

Set by Words & Graphics Ltd.
Anstey, Leicestershire
Printed and bound in Great Britain by
T. J. International Ltd., Padstow, Cornwall

This book is printed on acid-free paper

1

'Sarah, leave that cat alone.'

Three-years-old Sarah Kelly paused in her attempts to catch hold of 'Pompon' and regarded her mother with disfavour. Imelda Kelly, a thin sharp-featured blonde, gave her youngest a push up the steep flight of steps. Evading her mother's grasp, Sarah stuck her head against the railings and peered down into the area below, where the cat had found temporary refuge in the doorway of Nevin & Flood, Antiques.

'That cat'll scratch you,' Mrs Kelly warned, dragging Sarah in her wake. 'I told the Duffs they'd no business having it when there's kids in the house.'

This was a recurring grievance, nor was the younger Miss Duff's rejoinder quoted, it being to the effect that she and her sister had been in occupation long before the Kellys had returned to live with Mrs Kelly's parent; a temporary

1

arrangement necessitated by the behaviour of absconding Mr Gabriel Kelly.

Little Sarah led the way into the two-roomed hall flat, and Imelda pushed open the door to find her father seated in his shabby armchair, his feet extended before a blazing fire. A thin carpet covered the floor and the furniture also had seen better days. Joe Gallagher, who looked over sixty, had wispy grey hair and a careworn expression. He now laid aside his newspaper as if prepared to meet a new crisis.

'What's up?' he enquired.

Imelda banged her parcels on the table and began to remove her coat.

'It's that cat — you should have it out with the Duffs once and for all. You've been here quite as long as they . . . '

'Pompon?'

No more inappropriate name could have been devised for a scrawny animal with wedge-shaped head, enormous eyes and projecting teeth, one canine of which was missing so that the tongue protruded and slewed a little to the left. However some twelve years earlier, as an undersized kitten, she had possessed a short bushy tail — hence the title.

Joe Gallagher went on: 'If you keep the kids away, the cat won't touch them. She only scratches when they tease.'

'I've enough to do, Dad, without watching them every five minutes. What time is it? I'd better collect the others from school.'

Her father heaved himself out of the chair. 'I'll go,' he said, 'you put your feet up. And Sarah can come with me.

'It's early, and we'll go around by the canal; she likes that.'

He paused, then went on slowly: 'I know things are tough for you, girl, since Gabriel went, but no use making bad worse. The kids have taken a knock too.' He made a grimace. 'Maeve won't talk about him and Donal frets, and even Sarah keeps asking when he's coming back.'

'Do you think I don't ask myself the same question! Dad, you don't know, you can't, what it means. You and Ma . . . '

Imelda broke off and Mr Gallagher whose memories of his dead wife were

3

not unmixed with bitterness, said nothing to dispel the rosier picture evidently cherished by his daughter. Instead, he ventured to enquire if Gabriel had sent any money.

'Not for a good bit, and what he did send we couldn't live on. If it weren't for you taking us in, Dad, and the Social Welfare . . . Don't think I'm not grateful; this place wasn't meant for five,' she went on quickly, 'and you're all cramped in the one room, and if the landlord . . . '

The landlord, whose agent collected weekly rents, had been kept in ignorance of the Kelly invasion, and as yet no other tenant had apparently voiced a complaint.

Joe seized his opportunity: 'God love you, it's no trouble to me. It's like the old days again, and Donal and myself do have grand talks man-to-man. I always missed not having a son. Don't worry any more about the landlord. That's all settled up.'

'How?'

'Oh, a word in the right ear,' replied Mr Gallagher, reaching for his coat and tweed cap and wrapping a long woolly scarf around his throat, 'and a bit extra on the side, for the time being. I haven't lived here all these years not to know what goes on. *And* there's a rumpus starting about the couple overhead. If they get pushed out, or rather *she* does — not that I've anything against her, she's a quiet little one — anyhow, if they get the push, we're in line for the flat; me to move up and you and the kids to have this to yourselves.'

'Dad! You mean the piano player?'

This description did not do justice to the lady in question, a rising young pianist the backbone of a trio comprising piano, violin and 'cello. When the trio gave a recital, most of the rehearsals took place overhead, but no outright criticisms had been levelled until it was discovered that the violinist had in fact 'moved in'. Miss Duff then protested strongly, first to the parties themselves and, on being rudely rebuffed, finally to the agent. Initially, she received some support from the occupier of the back room on that floor, a Mrs Nevin, who had also spoken to the girl, but for the past week Mrs Nevin had been hospitalized as a result of minor injuries received in a traffic accident, and Annie Duff had continued the campaign alone.

Joe Gallagher now put on his gloves and took Sarah by the hand. 'Leave this to me,' he warned his daughter, 'and don't go upsetting the Duffs. Annie may be a bit of a tartar, but she's a decent old bird, and as for the sister . . . ' here Mr Gallagher's vocabulary broke down . . . 'well, just don't upset them,' he ended.

With this pronouncement, the door closed on grandfather and granddaughter, Sarah shouting ecstatically as they went in the direction of the canal.

Number 49 Organ Place, the scene of these and other later stranger events, had been built in the Dublin of 1772, and comprised four storeys above basement, together with a small attic. Organ Place was originally a wide rectangle, but the passage of time, decay, and late nineteenth century development had left its six remaining terraced houses (still numbered 45 to 50 inclusive) with a vista only of high walls and rear exits, though upper-floor windows still afforded pleasant views of the Grand Canal.

The history of number 49 was as follows. For over a hundred years it descended through three generations of the same family; well-to-do merchants who carefully maintained their property. Then, in the eighteen eighties, the last of the family died and the house was sold, its pristine condition enabling it to emerge relatively unscathed from the neglect of the next twenty years or so, after which a charitable institution purchased both it and number 50 and retained the two houses for another forty years. The institution then moving to modern premises, number 50 in which its offices had been located, was rented out in office units, and 49 let in furnished flats and bed-sittingrooms, the combined income still accruing to the charity who later sold these interests, so that to the modern tenant it was not always apparent who the present owner was — a cause for relief in one case and of frustration in others.

'You don't think they could actually

put us out?' Elizabeth asked anxiously of a florid young man of medium height, who was at that moment toasting bread on the end of a fork.

He looked up. 'Presumably, the object would be to get rid of me; general belief being that I seduced if not actually forced my way in upon you, and you're too gentle to give me the push.'

Elizabeth flushed. 'Nasty old cats,' she answered wrathfully.

'To which cat do you refer, my sweet? The rat-catcher in need of some dental repairs or the tall angular bespectacled . . . '

In spite of her anxieties, Elizabeth dissolved into laughter. 'Oh Ruairi, if they could hear you!'

Ruairi Mitchell rose from a kneeling position in front of the open fire, and deftly dislodged a slice of toast on to a pile keeping warm in the hearth. He lifted the plate and carried it to the table. Elizabeth had meanwhile been pouring the tea.

'I wonder who really owns this place?' she continued.

'Probably some big company,' he responded absently, his mouth full. 'Don't bother about it; we'll move when we have to.'

The red glow of the fire was the only illumination, and Elizabeth moved across to the windows to draw the curtains before putting on the lights. Outside, it had turned cold and there was rain forecast.

'I should hate to leave this place,' she said at length, her glance taking in the shabby chairs grouped round the fire, her piano next to the far window and, close to where they now sat, the cooking arrangements in one corner. The room, a large one, had been the drawing-room of the original Georgian residence; the ceiling still retained its fine plaster-work and there was a handsome fireplace.

Ruairi's gaze followed hers, and he eyed her speculatively. 'Pussies love places more than people,' he said. 'If it comes to a choice between me and the room, which will you give up?'

'Are you calling me a cat?'

'Meow. I thought we agreed that

description applied only to the Duffs — or rather, to Annie — and of course to our friend next door,' he jerked his thumb in the direction of the room behind him, occupied by Mrs Nevin.

'She's quite nice really,' Elizabeth said.

'Who? Annie?'

'No. Denise Nevin.'

'What did she want poking her nose in for then? It's no business of hers. Typical, of course, of the woman to be taken up with our concerns and then she can't look after herself. When I heard what happened to her, I couldn't help laughing.'

'Ruairi! She might have been badly hurt; luckily she got out of the way in time. As it was, she got a bang on the head and a wrist fracture. The car didn't even stop.'

'Serves her right, anyhow,' he growled, and reached for the teapot.

Elizabeth regarded him with a troubled expression. 'I wish you wouldn't say things like that; it only puts people off. Even Constance Duff was quite nice to me before you had the row with Annie . . . '

'What! Our grande dame?'

'She spoke to me about your playing, how she admired the . . . '

'And what would she know about it?' he interrupted rudely.

'She said when she lived in Paris she knew several composers and musicians.'

He cocked a derisive eyebrow: 'Mozart?'

Elizabeth laughed: 'She's pretty ancient, I know.'

Ruairi got up and went to sit at the piano. His hands spread out over the keys, he tried one or two notes and then struck a few chords and began to sing in a rather harsh voice the opening lines of Mozart's tenor aria:

'*Hier soll ich dich denn sehen, Konstanze* . . . '

The singing could be heard on the floor above.

Later, in the cold and wet of the raw November evening when the last remnants of the day's workers were seeking the comforts of hot food and a fire and in that half-hour before others, entertainment bound, took to the streets again, Denise Nevin paused at the narrow entrance to Organ Place.

Such a nuisance leaving hospital late in the day. She lived alone and her business partner had been away travelling all week. He might return tomorrow. At the hospital they put her into a taxi but passing through the city centre she remembered her cold empty flat and the lack of necessary supplies. Instructing the driver to deposit her at a local store close to home, she clambered out awkwardly, her fractured wrist still in plaster and strapped in position. It seemed pointless to retain the taxi for just a short trip round the block, and not until she reemerged from the shop with a plastic bag containing milk, sausages, rashers and a half-dozen eggs did she begin to think badly of this piece of economy.

The rain was not heavy, but it was persistent. Leaving the canal behind her, she walked slowly homewards hampered by her purchases, an overnight bag, and her useless arm still quite painful. At the entrance to Organ Place she halted for a moment, and shifting her bags into a more comfortable position, began to walk in the direction of number 49. She could see the shutters on the window of Nevin & Flood, Antiques. The shop had been closed all week of course, although Joe Gallagher had promised to take in any mail and keep an eye on the place generally. Unfortunate that Tony should have been away this week. She had tried contacting him at Nenagh, but he had left before her call came through. Well, only a little further now.

She did not hear, neither did she see the sure-footed dark figure whose steps followed hers. Only at the last second did she turn and instinctively raise the arm holding the bags. *I am a dead woman*, she thought, screaming and screaming. The eggs fell victims to the first blow.

2

Joe Gallagher was explaining, for the benefit of the Garda Siochana, his part in the events of the night before. At ten in the morning, the outer office of a large city police station also contained a number of other citizens: ranging from the tall seedy-looking man twisting a key ring round one finger and delivering his information out of the side of his mouth and in an undertone, to a rather agitated woman in a thick tweed skirt, Aran sweater, green stockings and red knitted hat, whose protests filled the room.

Pale winter sunlight streamed through the long windows and made patterns on the floor, and Joe felt its warmth penetrate his thin coat as he and the Sergeant settled themselves in a smaller room and faced one another across a desk.

'What time was this?' Sergeant O'Keeffe was asking.

'About seven — maybe a bit later. I'd been listening to the news on the radio, and then switched it off.'

'Was anyone with you?'

'My daughter was in the back room, with the three children; the youngest was in bed, and the other two doing their lessons.'

'She didn't hear anything?'

'The door was shut. I asked her, but she said the first she knew something was wrong was me outside in the street. I shouted, you see.'

'What attracted your attention?'

'Well, I knew it was a woman's screams, and it didn't sound like larking about.'

The Sergeant wrote that down, and then enquired: 'You ran outside?'

'I opened the front door and went out to the top of the steps. It was dark just there, but with the door open, the lights from the hall showed up a bit of the street below.'

'Did you see anything?'

'No — not then. The screaming had stopped. Just below me, outside the

15

basement window, I heard a bit of movement.'

'Did anyone else in the house come out?'

'They probably didn't hear anything; radios and TVs going full blast.'

Sergeant O'Keeffe, a tall burly man of around thirty-five, nodded and continued writing. 'Well, what happened next?'

'I went back into my own place and grabbed a rolled-up umbrella from off the back of the door. Then I went down the steps calling out who was there? I could hear footsteps then and they seemed to be going away — running. I kept calling, and when I got to the bottom of the steps I stood there and waited. Then I heard her moaning.'

'Mrs Nevin?'

'Yes. Poor woman, she'd only just come out of hospital, and her arm all in plaster.' Mr Gallagher ran a forefinger across the end of his nose, and went on: 'She was down in a heap outside the door to her shop; whether the fellow threw her in there or lay in wait and attacked her at the door, I can't say.'

'Can you describe the man?' asked the Sergeant, hoping for some real information. However, he was to be disappointed.

'I don't know what he *looked* like,' Mr Gallagher replied quickly. 'In fact, I hardly saw him, just an outline as he made off.'

'You are sure it was a man?'

'Well, yes,' Joe Gallagher seemed surprised. 'Wouldn't be a woman; not that kind of thing.'

The Sergeant gave him a penetrating look. 'Why, what exactly do you mean?'

But Joe didn't seem to mean anything other than women didn't go around bashing other women, and Sergeant O'Keeffe, whose fifteen years experience in the force had left him with a less chivalrous viewpoint, merely accepted this without comment, and requested his informant to go on with the narrative.

'Well, as I said,' responded Joe, 'she was down outside the door in a heap. There's three steps down, and she may have fallen and hit her head. She had parcels and a bag on her arm, and they were all on top of her. I had to get them off, and then I realized it was Mrs Nevin. She was giving little moans all the time. Well, I didn't like to leave her while I went for help, so I shouted and shouted, and of course Imelda, that's my daughter, well, she came out to see what was wrong . . . '

Here Mr Gallagher paused for breath, before continuing:

'Imelda didn't know what had happened, and I called up to her to phone for the police and an ambulance, only of course she straightaway ran down the steps crying out was *I* all right? I was just telling her to get back, when along comes Mr Mitchell, so I asked him to phone, which he did.'

The Sergeant, writing at full speed, hastily enquired: 'Is Mr Mitchell a neighbour of yours?'

'His young woman lives in the flat overhead mine.'

'You mean he was visiting her?'

'He was on his way in, yes.'

The Sergeant then asked for the young woman's name and on being told it was Miss Buckley, duly wrote that in his book.

He also made some enquiries about Mrs Nevin's family.

'She's a widow,' responded Mr Gallagher, 'her husband died two or three years ago — very sudden. He was only forty, or forty-five at most.'

'Do you know if there are any children; we haven't been able to contact relatives as yet.'

'She hasn't any kids. No parents either. Her mother died some years back. As far as I know, she was an only child. What about her partner? Maybe he could help.'

'Oh yes — Mr Flood. We are finding it difficult to trace the gentleman. Apparently he's away travelling for the firm.'

Joe nodded wisely. 'Usually comes back on a Thursday,' he said, 'so he'll probably be back today.'

There did not seem to be much more Mr Gallagher could tell the police, and having himself obtained the information that Mrs Nevin, suffering from concussion and multiple bruising, was in that condition officially described as 'comfortable', her rescuer returned to number 49.

The hall-door standing open, he passed through. Once inside he paused and gazed around as if seeing the interior with new eyes; noting the floor covering of which the basic colour, red, remained although the pattern had long since been trodden away; the uncovered stairs and dirty pale-green walls with, overhead, dingy flaking plaster. At the back of the hall, completing the picture of general depression, there was a combined bathroom and WC, the cistern of which was never entirely silent. Joe Gallagher wished and not for the first time, that his grandchildren might live elsewhere.

Sounds of animated female discussion drew him to his own door and a rather tired smile spread across his features as he recognized two voices, each striving for the mastery. He walked in to find his daughter dispensing tea and at the same time airing views hotly disputed by an elderly lady in grey, while two other young women looked on and little Sarah sat in their midst delighted with the company.

'Grampy!' shouted the last-named,

running over and flinging herself round his knees, her usual form of welcome. Decidedly, he might wish the children in better surroundings, but to him their presence had brought a new existence. How Gabriel could . . . His lips tightened, and Imelda pausing in her tirade, observed this expression and misunderstood it.

'Sarah! Leave your granddad alone.'

'Ah, don't bother the child,' he said, annoyed. 'Come here to me, pet.' He swung her up into his arms, and she crowed with delight.

The younger of the two girls now rose, making as if to depart. This was Frances, a social worker who occupied a small bed-sitter on the top floor.

'Just going, Mr G.,' she said briskly. 'Thanks for the tea, Imelda.' Turning again to Joe, she continued: 'I've been hearing about poor Mrs Nevin — any more word about her?'

Joe Gallagher repeated what he had been told.

'Poor soul,' responded Frances, with the ready sympathy of her profession, 'I'll telephone the hospital later on. They may let me see her. Well, I must be off. Coming Janet?'

This last was addressed to a pretty, dark-haired, rather quiet American, seated behind Miss Duff and absorbing 'atmosphere' as she herself would have put it. Obviously used to high standards, to move into a second-floor bed-sitter must have called for some sacrifice, but Janet Brown, researching into the background and culture of nineteenth century literary Ireland, offered no comment beyond saying she sure was lucky in coming on a house so exactly suited, the absence of hot water or a shower being hardly to be wondered at in such an interesting relic of the past. She occupied the room next to the Miss Duffs who were, Joe Gallagher suspected, of even more interest to the researcher than the house.

As Janet now left, having politely thanked her hostess for the tea, which she had not enjoyed but had drunk as one in duty bound to savour the experience, Annie Duff said as the door closed behind the two:

'Such nice young girls. Frances, of course, is a bit rough-spoken sometimes, but I'm sure no one could be pleasanter or kinder than Miss Brown. She's always offering to do errands or messages for myself and my sister.'

Joe grinned to himself, but Imelda took this in bad part. 'She's plenty of time on her hands,' she said.

Annie drew herself up (if it were possible for her to sit any straighter): 'My dear Mrs Kelly,' she began stiffly, 'I have no doubt the girl is actuated by motives of kindness, not but that my sister Constance has been able to provide her with most valuable information, so Miss Brown says.'

She rose from her chair and gathered her shopping things. 'Thank you for the tea, Mrs Kelly. You are very kind.'

Imelda was not quite mollified, but she muttered something to the effect that it was no trouble. Joe held open the door and Sarah, perched on his shoulder, waved bye-bye to Annie, whose grim old eyes softened as she took the child's hand in hers.

'The little pet,' she observed sentimentally. Sarah then made a grab for the gold-rimmed spectacles and had to be restrained, but Miss Duff laughed good-humouredly and with a sigh of relief Joe closed the door behind her and put Sarah down again.

'What brought that crowd in?' he enquired of his daughter.

'You may well ask,' she replied with a sniff. 'Nosy lot. Not Frances, though.' Here Imelda paused.

'If you want to know, *she* came about Gabriel. She thinks she can do something for us — me and the kids, I mean. She was just telling me, when the Duff one showed up with Janet Brown in tow. Annie, of course, only came to hear about last night. She asked for you; you should have seen her face when I told her where you were! Couldn't wait for you to get back so she could hear all the news!'

Imelda clattering the teacups together into a basin as she spoke, then went to put on a kettle to do the washing-up. Joe sank down into his armchair, and Sarah got into his lap and curled herself up comfortably. In a few minutes, she had fallen asleep. Observing the child, her mother's expression softened and Joe smiled as he gently stroked Sarah's hair.

'Tired out with all the excitement,' he said. 'And her granddad is suffering from reaction. I tell you when I went down those steps last night, I didn't know but I was coming to grips with some young thug — and if he hadn't run off like he did, who knows but it could be me laid up in the hospital!'

'You'd wonder he'd attack her so near the house; down at the end of the street there's only the blank wall and the gates opposite. Why do it just outside the door?' his daughter questioned reasonably.

'Perhaps he was trying to grab her keys — to get into the shop?'

'Yes, but look Dad,' Imelda said quickly, her sharp brain seizing on a number of objections, 'listen, she was coming out of hospital — right? How could anyone know when she'd arrive, if at all. And most likely she'd have someone with her, or come in a taxi anyhow.'

'She was sent home in a taxi,' Joe said.

'She must have let it go when she went to buy some provisions. If we'd only known she was coming, we could have got something in for her.'

'That's just the point, Dad. Did anyone know? Would a fellow hang around on chance, on a cold wet evening? He'd be better off breaking into the shop while she was away.' Imelda took a fresh dishcloth from the rack and began drying energetically.

'Dad!' she exclaimed.

Joe looked up, startled. 'What?'

Still clutching the dishcloth, and with a saucer in one hand, she came over to his chair and lowered her voice. 'You don't think the other could have been the same thing, do you?'

Joe looked at his daughter, but said nothing.

'I mean the accident she had,' Imelda went on, and then as her father still offered no comment, she shrugged. 'I suppose you'd say that was a daft idea!'

'On the contrary,' responded Joe reluctantly, 'I was just thinking the same thing myself.'

3

In a crowded hotel lounge a man sat in one corner. Several empty glasses stood on the table in front of him. Occasionally he glanced across to the large old-fashioned clock which hung above the door. Presently, he rose and went out to the lobby where he made a phone call. The girl at the desk knew him and spoke to him.

'Evening Mr Flood,' she said. 'Haven't seen you for quite a while now.'

The man responded easily and drifted in her direction. She was small and rather plump with dark hair and a ready flow of conversation. As she chatted carelessly, her small shrewd eyes flitted over the man standing in front of her, noting the easy assurance, the well-fitting clothes, the two gold rings with the third left-hand finger conspicuously bare and, over-all, the dominant masculinity which made its impression even on her fairly cast iron sensibilities.

The claims of a woman guest she blatantly ignored until the woman became unpleasant, when with an air of martyred resignation the dark girl turned to her, relinquishing her hold on Tony Flood who ambled back to the lounge.

His table was no longer empty. It was now occupied by a nondescript man of forty-odd who gazed thoughtfully at Mr Flood as the latter approached. Both remained silent until the bigger man was seated. Then the newcomer said:

'Brought it?'

'No.' Tony offered his companion a cigarette and lit one himself.

'You're a damn fool.'

'Maybe.'

'When?'

'Things are a bit sticky just now. I'll have to have more time.'

The nondescript man absorbed this without comment, merely tapping his cigarette against the glass ash-tray. At length he said: 'What'll I tell my principal?'

'Just that.'

'Won't do. You said a week and you've had three.'

'It's not a supermarket!'

The small man looked at him queerly. 'Not got cold feet? If you have, think of your own position, that's my advice.'

'Is that a threat?'

'Use your head.' There was contempt in the colourless voice.

'OK, OK. I take your point. Anyway I don't *want* to back out.'

'Right,' said the small man, 'what'll I say?'

'Say I won't fail, but it has to be in my own time. I'm the one taking the risk, remember.'

'Small risk.'

'Would you do it?'

The nondescript man grimaced. 'Maybe,' he said, 'if the price was right.'

'I'll bet,' said Tony.

★   ★   ★

Denise Nevin had returned to number 49. A fair-haired woman, her rather attractive features marred by some discolouration and with her wrist still in plaster, she looked pale and nervous.

A fire had been lit in anticipation of

the occupant's homecoming, and the ever-willing Frances was just pulling forward a chair and assisting Denise to remove her coat, when a knock on the door proclaimed the arrival of Janet.

'I hope you don't think I'm butting in,' said that girl, as she stuck her small dark head round the door.

Denise, not long acquainted with the young American, looked rather surprised, but Frances said briskly: 'Come on and make yourself useful.'

'Delighted! My dear Mrs Nevin, I was that upset when I heard what had happened. So many people being mugged these days!'

Denise giggled hysterically, and Frances eyed her with concern. 'What is it?'

'It's just that I hadn't thought of myself as being 'mugged'.' She gave another giggle and then recollected herself, forestalling an apology from Miss Brown. 'I don't really remember much; it was dark and it happened so quickly.'

'Didn't you see anything?' asked Frances.

Denise swept her fair wavy hair away from her face.

'I think I sort of half-turned — I must have heard someone close behind me. I remember putting up an arm to shield my face, and I suppose my parcels got in the man's way. And of course I screamed my head off. Luckily Joe Gallagher heard and came running.'

'Do you think you could identify the man?'

Denise shook her head. 'The police asked me that,' she said. 'I couldn't even say definitely that it *was* a man; I don't think he was very tall. Anyway, I never saw his face.'

Janet, who had been occupied with domestic tasks, now came forward with a tea-tray and some scones which she had brought with her.

'Fresh from the oven, Mrs Nevin,' she said with a smile. They were indeed hot, smothered in butter and tasted delicious.

'This is very good of you two,' Denise said as she lay back in her chair sipping tea and watching the tall flames leap up in the chimney. The curtains were not yet drawn, and through the long window she could see the branches of a tree, already bare and black against the November sky, and behind the tree, rear windows of other similar houses.

She rejoined the conversation in time to hear Janet's transatlantic accent disclaiming any virtue.

'We're just the first contingent, Mrs Nevin,' Janet murmured gently.

'What do you mean?'

'Why, the Miss Duffs wanted to be the first to welcome you, only they had to visit their brother this afternoon. They go every Sunday. He's blind and an invalid and lives in a home, so they don't care to miss going . . . '

'They said to be sure to tell you they'd see you this evening,' Frances interjected, 'but I said you might be too tired. You probably need a rest.'

'My head still feels rather peculiar,' Denise admitted, 'but otherwise, apart from my wrist, I'm all right. I'm very fond of the Duffs — especially Constance.' Denise roused herself a little. 'You don't mean,' she went on, 'that Constance travels all that way to visit the brother — why she's older than he is.'

'She tells me she is eighty-seven,' Janet confirmed, 'Annie must be a younger person altogether. I believe Constance is the eldest of her family.'

'You've been devoting a lot of time to her,' Frances said with a smile.

Janet shook her dark curls, and her dainty hand reached out for another scone.

'I've been well repaid,' she answered, 'as I expect you've guessed. Constance is a *person* and she has the most wonderful memory — you just wouldn't believe! She tells me about her years in Paris. And afterwards she worked in Dublin and she's made dresses for so many interesting women, and she remembers their names and if they were married — most of them were, I suppose the unmarried ones in those days weren't so interested in how they looked,' so saying, Janet pushed a last piece of scone into her small mouth, and wiped her hand in a paper napkin.

I wonder who made the dress *you're* wearing, Denise thought to herself, giving the American girl's outfit casual appraisal.

The heavy jersey-knit dress with its high collar and long sleeves fitted the wearer like a glove. But Janet was continuing to expound on her researches:

'One or two of these old ladies still visit with Constance. She doesn't design now, of course, but she and Annie make up garments that these old ladies like. I met one of them. I called during an afternoon and there was this *incredible* person, looking about a hundred. How she climbed the stairs, I'll never know! Her hands were simply covered with rings, and she talked and talked. Constance very kindly asked me to stay, and when I finally left I straightway rushed up to my room so I could get it all down on paper. The things that woman had seen! Why, as a child she had been at the funeral of Parnell!'

Frances, with little interest in affairs of long ago and who in any case had heard this story before, now made an effort to turn the conversation, but Janet was not to be diverted.

'Do you know that Constance and Annie have an antique sewing machine? It has a wheel with a sort of pulley, and an iron foot-plate. It is Annie who uses the machine — Constance sews by hand.' In tones of one repeating a lesson, Janet ended on a rising note.

Denise laughed. 'Those old sewing machines are still quite common. As a matter of fact, I sold the Duffs the one they have now; their previous model gave out and I picked up another at an auction. It was in good condition and not much used. Annie didn't fancy going electric.'

'It's all terribly interesting,' the American girl said. 'I don't know how I came to be so lucky as to find myself in a place like this. I suppose you know a lot about antiques?' and Janet looked wistful.

Rightly judging this to be an opening gambit, Denise smiled. 'Perhaps you'd like to come through the shop some time, Miss Brown . . . '

'Janet!' said that person eagerly. 'I'd just love to.'

'Well, I should warn you it's none of it really first class. Of course there are pieces which might be of interest to you in your work — particularly the furniture. We have quite a lot of mahogany stuff, as well as brass bedsteads; they fetch good prices now, and Leo cleans and polishes them for us.'

'You mean the old man with the pushcart?' queried the American.

Frances gave a snort. 'Don't let him hear you,' she said, 'he wouldn't like that description of himself.'

Denise smiled. 'No, indeed.'

'Why, what have I said?'

'He does have a cart, I admit,' answered Frances, 'but he's not that old; not more than fifty, anyway.'

'I don't think he's quite that even,' Denise said. 'My husband, Andrew, was about the same age.'

'Has he been here long; Leo, I mean?' Frances enquired hastily, anxious to get away from what might prove to be a depressing subject.

'Oh I think so — in fact, I can't remember a time when he didn't live here.'

'He has the room next to mine,' Frances explained to Janet, who replied that she had met him a few times on the stairs.

'You should try to cultivate him,' Denise said, glancing at the American. 'I'm sure he's quite as interesting as either of the Miss Duffs.'

'Now you're laughing at me,' Janet protested.

Denise murmured that she had no such intention.

Without warning, the noise of rapid-fire arpeggios suddenly burst upon them from the adjoining room, and Frances got up with a wrathful expression saying:

'She might show *some* consideration! She must know you're home again and not feeling too grand. I'll just go and have a word . . . '

'No — please,' Denise responded urgently, 'there has been some unpleasantness and I'd rather not add to it. There's only the thin partition between us; originally this was all one room. Elizabeth doesn't realize how the sound carries.'

'You can hear her at the top of the house,' Frances continued belligerently, as scales succeeded the arpeggios.

'Well, it *is* her career; she must practice somewhere.'

'Yes, but it goes on all day,' replied Frances, whose work sometimes called for odd hours. 'Old Simms next to me does his share of banging and hammering but, decent enough, when I told him I was working nights, he said he wouldn't disturb me and he doesn't now. Though when Janet's room was vacant, I did half-think of moving, but hers is at the back of the house and I rather enjoy my view of the canal.'

'You may like to think again of moving,' said Janet with a smile, 'my time here will soon be up. I'm due back in the States for Christmas and I rather want to do Europe before I leave.'

'A holiday would be lovely,' Frances agreed enviously. 'How would you manage about your stuff though? You wouldn't want to cart it around Europe.'

'Janet can store it with us if she likes,' Denise said. 'Plenty of room at the back of the shop. Entirely at her own risk of course,' she added with a grimace. 'We do get the odd rat.'

'Rats!' Janet shuddered.

'Well, Pompon caught one recently. With the canal so close, there's bound to be a few about.'

Janet still looked upset.

Denise was all at once very tired, and wished her visitors would go. As the conversation continued, she took less part in it, and presently Frances said they must be leaving and the patient should have an early night.

'I'll leave a note for the Duffs,' she added, 'you won't want another lot of visitors later on.'

Afterwards, as Denise lay in bed with only the firelight for company, the sounds of piano practice ceased and Mr Ruairi Mitchell took up his violin and began to play, not scales or arpeggios, but dreamy and contemplative Mendelssohn. Her senses lulled, she floated away into restful slumbers.

4

The concert hall was slowly filling up. It was not large, holding perhaps five hundred persons, and as the musicians were not very well known, unlikely to be crowded.

Mr Leo Simms, arriving early and taking up a central position, looked around with satisfaction. His ticket had not cost much; his seat was a good one and reasonably comfortable; the central heating kept him nicely warm (in choosing his seat he had carefully avoided the draught coming from a side exit) and in addition he would enjoy the music even should its performance prove less than perfect.

A square-shaped man, his bulk made him appear shorter than he really was. His feet were unexpectedly small and his hands, long since roughened by coarse work and exposure, still expressive. His face showed a cosmopolitan ancestry, much of it Hebrew.

When his father, Maxi Symmanouski, had left a Baltic port many years before, bound for America, the vessel carrying the Symmanouski family had been uncomfortable, not to say unseaworthy. After a hazardous spell at sea and a number of unscheduled ports of call, the ship had put into Queenstown, now Cobh, and Maxi had staggered ashore determined to sail no further and leaving his parents and other relatives to continue their journey across the Atlantic.

He finally reached Dublin, where the members of his own community were kind to him and gave him temporary financial assistance. Meanwhile, out on the Atlantic the elderly vessel carrying his entire family foundered and sank one night, leaving no survivors. Maxi Symmanouski had become an orphan.

He stayed in Dublin and he worked hard. He repaid the money borrowed and then secured a loan to set him up in a small way of business. The business prospered and eventually he married a young woman with a little money, and the couple had several children the youngest of whom was Leopold.

Quite early on, the older children showed promise. Just as their father had worked hard, so they also persevered, and in the course of time emerged from school and university with high honours, subsequently filling a number of important positions.

A gap of eight years separated Leo from his next elder brother, but he showed no disposition to follow the example set him. Considered either lazy or stupid by his father, who by this time was getting on in years, he seldom went to school but spent most of his time wandering about the city picking up odds and ends which he used to store in a shed at the bottom of the garden, nicknamed by the family 'Leo's dump'.

When he was fourteen, his father died and his mother went to live with her only daughter, by that time married. The father's business was sold. After provision for his wife, his children inherited the shares left them. Leo's share was the smallest and until he was twenty-one he received only such sums as his family considered appropriate. What he did with this money or with his eventual inheritance, nobody knew.

His sister and her husband first took him to live with them; a considerable sacrifice on their part, for they lived in a smart neighbourhood. After some months, he parted from them and his mother, dividing his time between his two elder brothers. One of these then married and the other moved out of the country, and by the time he was sixteen Leo was living alone and in business for himself.

He acquired a handcart, which he trundled round the markets and old-clothes shops. This was the time of the Emergency, and the secondhand business flourished. Leo not only fed himself; it was generally supposed, even by his family, that he made money; and with the capital left him by his father and indeed with money which he could easily have borrowed, Leo might have become a prosperous businessman, as had his father before him.

But he borrowed no money. He never

bought or rented a shop. In an old and dilapidated part of the city, he had a yard containing a wooden shed. For a time he even lived in that shed, until one bad winter drove him out of it. In the early nineteen fifties, he took up residence in Organ Place in the room which he had occupied ever since, and around this time he began calling himself Simms. He never married of course.

He now settled himself more comfortably, having removed his overcoat and cap, which revealed naturally curling grey hair of fine quality and still abundant. As he waited for the performance to commence, he noted the arrival of other members of the audience; familiar faces, some of these, at this and other concert halls. He was in the middle of a row and a group of schoolchildren came in and filled up the seats on his left and in front. To his right were a number of earnest middle-aged women, a young student with big feet and a bush of hair, and a rather alarming lady of sixty, made-up in the style of her youth.

The seat next to his remained vacant

until, just as the lights were being extinguished, another heavily-built man got in, disturbing the ladies and drawing a grunt of anguish from the student who had not bothered to rise and had his feet squashed as a result. The latecomer then divested himself of his coat, being still on his feet when the musicians came onto the platform to be greeted by mild applause.

The first item on the programme was a sonata for violin and piano, and Leo nodded approval as Ruairi Mitchell strode forward with an assured air and with a firm grip raised the violin to his chin and tucked it underneath. Meanwhile, Elizabeth Buckley, accompanied by a timid little girl, settled themselves at the piano. The timid child's function was of course to turn the pages of the music.

Ruairi glanced round to see if all were ready, and the performance began. Leo, to whom the music was already familiar (as it was to everyone at number 49) observed the players' techniques. The violinist wrapped himself in music-making, sparing little thought (apparently) for the piano accompaniment. He seldom glanced at his partner but rather left it to her to keep in touch with him. Both soloists played from music and during the last movement — marked *Allegro molto* but taken at a pace suggestive of *Presto* — the harassed child who turned the pages for the pianist had apparently been bidden to leap up and turn one page for the violinist also, at the crucial moment when he was unable to take his bow from the instrument. To Mr Simms, familiar with the piece and slightly amused at the tempo, this manoeuvre came as no surprise, but the child's anxious face as she glanced from one performer to the other suggested she was aware it required a skill and experience she did not possess.

Leo chuckled to himself, causing his neighbour to turn round in some surprise. The disaster was not long in coming. At the beginning of a particularly difficult passage for both piano and violin, Elizabeth took her eyes from the music and nodded violently to the child, who shot up in alarm and promptly fell over the leg of the chair. The impetus carried her forward even as the chair fell with a crash, and her outstretched hand, ready to turn the all-important page, instead caught the violinist's music-stand and projected it — tripod, music and all — into the audience.

There was a moment of shock and then several things happened at once. As the unfortunate girl, unable to save herself, fell to the floor and the schoolchildren dissolved into helpless nervous laughter, the pianist half-rose and made as if to come forward, but the violinist while continuing to play, turned towards her and (savagely) motioned her back.

Cries of concern came from the centre of the first two rows as tripod and music descended, but one quick-witted fellow jumped up and caught the stand so that it did no damage. The girl scrambled to her feet; she even made a tentative movement to take the tripod from the gentleman in the audience who held it out to her but glancing at the soloist for confirmation, recoiled, burst into tears and then fled incontinently from the stage. *Allegro molto* continued to its rousing finale, and

Mr Simms who had had a hard struggle not to give way to the laughter all around him, joined in the ensuing applause.

'Dear oh dear,' he said to the man sitting next to him, 'quite an eventful performance.' It was then he discovered the man was his cousin.

'Hello Leo,' said the man as the lights went up, 'didn't recognize you before in the gloom.'

Mr Simms who was not always recognized except by the members of his immediate family, turned a benign countenance towards the speaker.

'Haven't seen you for quite some time,' the cousin went on, and as Leo nodded agreement, he added: 'How's the brother these days?'

'You saw his picture in the papers?'

'Yes I did. Looked in splendid shape. He must be proud of the boy.'

'My father would have been very proud,' Mr Simms replied gravely, 'his grandson a surgeon!'

'Never knew the old man,' the cousin remarked. 'Bit of a patriarch, eh?'

'He was alone in the world. He had no

one except his wife and children; and my mother's family he did not always approve of.'

'I can understand why,' said the cousin, who belonged to that side of the family.

Mr Simms tactfully changed the subject. 'How is your own work, or should I ask?'

'I'm taking a break now, before the Christmas rush.'

'Ah yes, that is a busy time for you no doubt.'

The cousin lapsed into silence and presently Leo enquired: 'You are enjoying the concert?'

'Best entertainment I've seen for years.'

Leo smiled, but said reproachfully: 'I meant the . . . er, music, you know.'

'Not too much interested that way myself,' the cousin admitted. 'I like a good tune alright, though.' He glanced around hastily as if fearful this statement might have been overheard, but the seats behind him were vacant their occupants having gone in search of refreshments. 'The violinist seemed rather good,' he added.

'You thought so too? He is a neighbour of mine and I felt perhaps too much familiarity had made me partial. I liked the way he carried on just now *musically speaking* I mean. There was some improvisation at one point, very skilfully done.'

The cousin turned and regarded him. 'The family don't make half enough of you Leo,' he remarked cordially. 'Surprising, all that goes on inside that head of yours!'

Leo permitted himself a little smile. 'It was my father's regret that I was not clever. He said I reminded him of some relative of his who engaged in small trading ventures.'

'Whereas the truth is you're not stupid enough to join in the scramble like the rest of us!'

Mr Simms raised his fine brows. 'It is true I take a detached view sometimes, but that is my nature. I could not live in any other way. And indeed, my lodgings give much scope for human observation.'

'49 Organ Lane, eh?'

'Place — Organ Place.'

'Oh yes. I see you were in the news lately.'

'You mean Mrs Nevin?'

'Were you there when it happened?'

'No, I'm seldom home at that hour. A Mr Gallagher went to her assistance, and our violinist here was also on the scene.'

'The papers made no mention of him.'

Mr Simms looked amused. 'A disappointment for Mr Mitchell, perhaps. Publicity — it helps. Ah, we are about to begin the second half, I see.'

The hall which had filled up again now buzzed with conversation which died away as three musicians came onto the platform. During the interval, extra music-stands had been set out and the soloists, now joined by their 'cellist colleague, were to give a performance of Beethoven's Trio in B Flat Major, the 'Archduke'.

Even Mr Simms was surprised and pleased at the result. After the debacle of the first half, the players apparently felt nothing they now did could give a worse impression and accordingly adopted a relaxed approach. Although showing some rough edges and at times lack of cohesion, over-all it was a very creditable performance and one which provoked loud applause at the end.

As Leo left the hall, he remarked that he had enjoyed the evening.

'So did I,' admitted the cousin. 'It's early yet though. How about something to eat?'

Leo regretfully declined, remarking that he did not often eat out, and the cousin was at once apologetic.

'No use asking you to come to my place, then. Not that I do much cooking myself,' he added. 'Can't be bothered.'

'Perhaps you would care . . . if you would like to come back to Organ Place, we might have a meal together there.'

'Nothing I'd like better,' said the cousin cheerfully, and in the darkness Leo's face bore a wide smile.

They walked along through the busy lighted streets, and turning south they crossed the river. Leo had a shuffling gait and his companion a free stride, but neither appeared tired after several miles, nor did they converse much.

Although Organ Place was a cul-de-sac, several back lanes adjoined and by one of these routes Leo guided his relative towards the house. The front door was now firmly shut at all hours and Leo produced a key and then led the way upstairs.

To live at the top of such a house was to keep in good physical shape — or move. Even the cousin, accustomed to hard exercise, felt some constriction at the backs of the knees as he mounted the sixth and last flight of stairs. Or rather, it was not the last for one more led upwards from the top landing, ending at a door almost in the roof — the attic room.

'Who lives here, Leo?'

'On this landing, you mean?'

'Well yes. Suppose you want to slip out for a paper or a packet of fags; I bet you think twice about it!'

'Fortunately,' said Mr Simms gravely, 'I do not smoke.' He inserted a large old-fashioned key in the lock and opened the door. A fire burned low in the grate and he stirred it up and put on more fuel.

When they had consumed a meal,

surprisingly well-cooked by Mr Simms himself, and had settled into the two armchairs by the fire, Leo brought the conversation back to the subject of his neighbours.

'I have this front room here, and Frances Loughnane a very energetic and hard-working girl, she occupies the small front room next to mine. Across the landing, are Mr and Mrs Tracey, and in the attic room above . . . '

'What! Someone actually lives up there?'

'But yes, certainly.' Leo waved an expressive hand. 'In a very hot summer it is a little unpleasant perhaps. But the roof is good; it does not leak. The man who lives there has occupied it for several years.'

'And who is he?'

'He is Vincent Molesworth, the actor.'

'Never heard of him.'

Leo permitted himself a smile. 'I did not suppose you would have. He is mostly unemployed.'

'And is glad of a modest rent?'

'Something of the kind.'

Leo enjoyed a mild gossip about his neighbours and the next hour passed agreeably. Finally, the cousin said it was getting late and he'd better be going. 'Although,' he added, gazing rather enviously at the snug comfort around him, 'its hard to tear oneself away, it's been so pleasant.'

'But stay then!' Leo said at once.

'Oh well I couldn't — rather a lot of trouble for you,' the cousin replied but in the doubtful tones of one who only needs to be convinced.

'No trouble, no trouble,' Leo's voice was eager. 'I have a spare bed here — never use it.'

As he spoke he bent down and from under his own bed dragged out an old-fashioned iron bedstead in three sections. Seeing his cousin's cold eye fall on this heap of discomfort, he added hastily: 'For me of course — not for you.'

After some argument, the cousin gave way to these suggestions; the iron bed was erected (with apologies to Miss Loughnane who hammered on the wall, asking what the noise was about) and Leo fell asleep having secured from his guest a promise to stay for a couple of days.

5

That night a man received an urgent message. The small scrap of paper pushed under his barricaded door said:

'Not safe to come again. A friend taking this. They don't know him. Get out tonight and keep away. I've been watched since two days. There's stuff for your trip where we said. Good luck.'

The note was roughly printed and unsigned.

Michael listened. Whoever delivered the message had come silently and departed without noise. Michael read it again. His hand trembled and the scrap of paper fell to the floor. If he could believe it! Even if it were genuine, he would have to leave this shelter and go out in the cold and grapple once again with life as he had not done since he was a young man. He was sixty-seven, and fear had suddenly aged him.

'Dear God,' he said aloud, 'you'd think I was ninety.'

He ran a hand across his face and felt the stubbly grey beard. Since he'd been here he hadn't shaved, but the growth was slow. It wouldn't disguise him.

Should he go or should he stay?

The note (if genuine) said to go now and not look back. He sat down on the narrow bed and put his head in his hands. If his friend had written the note then he, Michael Doyle, was in real danger if he stayed where he was. If his friend had been taken and forced to write, or if the note were simply a forgery, then they knew enough to come for him at will but preferred to take him in the open.

His mind, long accustomed to reasoning in tight financial places, now took up the problem for him. How much food did he have? He got up and made a rapid count of the stores. With careful rationing he had enough for seven perhaps eight days. Add another few days with little or no food. If he had to, he could hole-up for near two weeks, although at the end of that time he would be in no shape to get away unaided; but he could stay, and his friend might get back to him again. That was possibility number one — right.

Next: Whelan might know of his whereabouts and be holding back — waiting. Whelan was not the prime mover. The brain which had conceived this whole plan was at once devious and subtle. Whelan was just the machine setting the wheels in motion as instructed. Yes, but machinery could be dangerous if left untended and it was just possible this had happened: Whelan left to act alone. And what about his, Michael's trump card displayed on that last day. They knew — they must know now. Unless death had freed him . . .

Better not think too much. He had to evolve a plan of action. He could do as the note said but if the note were false then to go and collect the cache was to walk into a trap. On the other hand, the very want of supplies might hinder his escape. He picked up the note again and reread the message. Where human reasoning failed, there was still instinct.

'I'll go,' he said aloud.

His decision made, at once he felt better. Before he left he must make certain arrangements. Burn that note, that was number one. He struck a match and the small scrap of paper ignited and shrivelled into dust. That was that.

He collected some tins of sardines and packets of cheese and stowed them away on his person. He had a bottle of whiskey, half-full, which he put in one overcoat pocket. In the other he carried his automatic. He placed all the remaining food in one cardboard carton. Then he took the blankets from the bed and folded them into a neat pile. To a casual observer the room should appear unoccupied. Refuse he planned to take out with him. If he failed to gain entrance to his next hiding place or if for any reason he was held up, he might yet make it back here. Rather than be stranded in the open, he would take that risk.

Removing the barricades from the door, cautiously he drew back the bolt and looked out. There was nothing to see of course for the corridor was unlit. If he had been followed or betrayed then he was as good as dead. If not, then — not. He could feel the sticky sweat of fear under his arms and at the base of the spine. He left the door ajar and moved out into the passage. Then he halted and listened. Only the muffled sounds of heavy traffic came from the street above.

He walked to the end of the corridor and turned to the left. There was a door — a back exit. It was bolted and the key was in the lock. Gently, very gently, he undid the bolts and turned the key. The door opened outwards and a short flight of steps led to a narrow yard. Lights from the street above penetrated some of the black density.

His left hand supported a plastic refuse sack in front of his torso, while the right hand closed on his automatic. Again moving very quietly, he pushed the door shut waiting for the lock to snap home. In the dark he could not be identified unless close to, nor would they risk getting the wrong man. He moved down the steps and across the yard, walking slowly. Then he waited and listened. He put his back to the wall still holding the sack in front of him.

Beside him was a small door, bolted

and with a heavy lock. Michael took stock of the situation. He was of medium height and weight and the wall was ten feet or so in height and was topped with barbed wire. He looked back at the door through which he had come. Should he retreat? Whoever delivered the message had left the building by another route obviously. As he stood there his inner voice said: you've got this far, don't turn back.

He laid the refuse sack down to the right of the door and stood on it. The tins rattled a bit, shifting around in the other waste matter compressed by his weight. He took a handkerchief from his pocket and wrapped it around his right hand. Then, running his left foot along the top of the bolt, he made a spring for the wire. He knew if he didn't make it at the first or second attempts then exhaustion would defeat him altogether, so he put all he had into that first spring and almost sobbed with relief as his hand found a grip.

The wire bent a little under his weight and it pulled out towards him, but he held on, getting purchase from the wall with his knees. His other hand grabbed for the wire also and was cut, but not badly. He stuck his right knee between the wire and the wall. There was no glass.

Desperation at his exposed position gave him new impetus. Still holding the wire, he managed to stand up. He got one leg over; then the other, tearing his clothes. Once over the wire, he knelt on the top of the wall and held on while one leg dangled; finally dropping to the ground in an untidy heap.

For a while he just lay there on his back — dazed. His shoulders hurt and he had hit his head in the fall. Also he seemed to have wrenched something.

Then he heard a car come up behind him. He scrambled to his feet, nearly crying with sudden pain. The headlights hit him full-on, and he blinked and put his hand up to shield his eyes. The other hand reached into his pocket for the gun.

The car stopped. Inside, were two men. They conversed, and then one pulled down the window and spoke to him, as he sidled along the wall.

'Hey there, you alright old son?'

Michael Doyle, with his tattered clothes, a whiskey bottle protruding from his pocket and a blood-stained hand held across the stubbly bearded face, made a pathetic figure.

'Thought you might have been hit,' the speaker went on. 'Sure you're OK?'

Michael nodded and edged away.

'Don't look as if you've had too much to eat lately,' the man continued, fumbling in his pockets. 'Here, get yourself a decent meal with this!' and he held out a crisp note.

Michael stared at him, and then at the note. Quite a few of its fellows nestled in his own breast-pocket, but he put out his hand, giving a little gasp as the upward movement jerked his arm.

'Thanks,' he muttered.

The man nodded, shut up the window, and the car moved away at speed.

Left to himself, Michael felt the sweat run down inside his clothes, but his legs carried him forward as if driven by their own propulsion. Emerging from the narrow side-turning, he turned left and shuffled along the street past brightly-lit shops. The hour was late but some of the shops were open and from bars and discos there came sounds of human activity and warmth, and the smell of instant food.

The man had been right. He, Michael Doyle, needed a decent meal; a hot meal with soup and meat. The fall seemed to have deadened his fears and he began to look for a suitable place. Some with teenage customers scared him off and in others he might have been known or, in his present condition, rejected.

At *Guido's Restaurant*, he paused. It was rather shabby. He gazed avidly at the menu card in its brass holder, and his eye fell on that magic word *Beef* . . . He was still hesitating when a police patrol car came on the scene, causing him to quickly step inside. No doubt the police were looking for him too; bound to be. And if they found him, what could he tell them? Unless he had proof, what could they do? Proof, or a reasonable suspicion. And if they were powerless, Whelan had only to wait. With Michael Doyle gunned down by nameless men, Whelan's attitude would be to give every assistance to the police and show kindness to the grief-stricken widow. Michael ground his teeth, and the rather plain waitress handing him a menu card looked concerned.

Almost without thinking, he had seated himself at a table. It was warm and friendly. There was a worn red carpet on the floor and facing him a row of empty wine bottles of different shapes hung along one wall. They were reflected in the long mirror opposite, in which Michael also saw his own reflection. It took him a few moments to recognize it, so decrepit had he become.

The girl was staring at him and afraid he might lose his chance of the meal he pulled out the note the man had given him and dropped it on the table.

'I can pay,' he said defiantly.

'What is your order?' she asked and as he gave it he read a pity in her eyes which brought sudden tears to his own. He turned away.

When she had gone, he looked around. There were not many customers at this hour; mostly men and one or two shabbily dressed. He began to feel better. He was warm again after weeks of cold. Before the food came, he struggled out of his coat and hung it up, first taking care to remove the automatic and slip it into his jacket pocket. He did this carefully, and no one seemed to notice.

There was a men's room, and he left his table and went inside. Discovering it to be unoccupied, he gave himself careful scrutiny in the mirror there. He looked about ten years older, feeble and dirty, and there was blood on his face and hand. The fall seemed to have numbed him and any sudden movement caused him pain. Already there appeared to be some bruising. He washed away the blood-stains, cleaning out the cuts with soap. For the rest, his clothes were torn and dirty and he smelt of stale sweat. However, on the credit side it would be hard to recognize in this bearded unkempt elderly man the wealthy company president of only weeks before.

He went back to his table. He was beginning to feel very sleepy but the food when it came revived him. It was good and well-cooked and the girl offered him another helping.

'There's no extra to pay,' she said.

He nodded silently, and presently she returned with the food.

' . . . very good of you,' he muttered.

'It's nothing,' she said and moved away.

It came to him then that she reminded him of Bernie. Where was Bernie now, he wondered? The mere mention of her name had paved the way for his escape. He ought to feel grateful. Instead, it was Kate he minded about. Odd though that thinking of Bernie should give him such a queer stab of — pain, almost.

He finished his meal and paid the check. Incredibly, there was even some change. He did not argue, but shuffled out quietly.

It was two hours later when he reached the cellar. He had walked, fearing to take a taxi and be recognized. The meal had given him energy at the start but after a while he was having to fight off a craving for sleep. He could have lain down on the concrete and slept. He plodded on and on, one foot in front of the other, his eyes unseeing. Had Whelan's men spotted him, he would not have stood a chance. But no one saw apparently.

The cellar was in a disused warehouse, and so tired was he that he went down into it without a thought of danger. He came on a bundle of old hessian bags in one corner, and without bothering to search further, slowly and painfully took off his coat, removed the bottle of whiskey and swallowed some, and then wrapping himself in the coat he lay down and fell into a deep sleep.

6

The following morning, a Saturday, there began at 49 Organ Place a large-scale row, originally between the Duffs, Ruairi Mitchell and the rent collector, but subsequently widening to embroil Imelda Kelly, Frances and Janet and (most unlikely of all) Mr Simms' cousin.

Now on Saturday mornings the rent collector was in the habit of calling at around ten o'clock. He also called to other flat dwellings in the area and this was his day for his 'regulars'. Other less prompt payers were tackled at different times during the week or month. At this hour on a Saturday, both Denise Nevin and her partner were usually to be found in their basement antique shop but the rent collector did not call there because the rent of the shop and also of Mrs Nevin's first-floor room was paid monthly by cheque. Neither did he knock on Joe Gallagher's door, for that man had recently paid several weeks' rent in advance.

Accordingly the collector, a Mr Harper, mounted to the first floor. Aged about forty-five, he was thin and spare and had a neat moustache. Elizabeth Buckley, at whose door he paused, had gone to the shops and a slip of paper giving that information protruded from under the mat. In the centre of the door, affixed by a single drawing-pin, was a white card bearing the instruction: 'Do not knock before 11.30 a.m.'

Now Mr Harper achieved many of his best results through simple curiosity. His employers were usually advised in good time of tenants likely to vanish into the night; of tenants guilty of wanton damage or of those tenants who sub-let contrary to agreement.

He had taken note of representations made to him about the presence of Ruairi Mitchell and had passed on those remarks to his employers who so far had given him no instructions. Miss Buckley paid regularly and he had no doubt if he came back the following week money would be forthcoming. But he *was* curious . . .

Ignoring the directions on the card, he knocked loudly. There was no reply and he banged again with his fist. This time he heard some movement and, encouraged, thumped vigorously in response.

The door opened abruptly and a man swathed in bed-clothes appeared. A sheet gaily patterned in daisies trailed behind him and around his shoulders was draped a pink woolly blanket and a multi-coloured quilt. However, the man's temper did not match his cheerful apparel.

'Are you illiterate?' he demanded acidly. 'Can you not read; are you blind, mentally deficient . . . '

'I've come for the rent.' The solid unemotional voice cut into the other's tirade. Ruairi broke off, then said shortly:

'Elizabeth's gone out. Call back at twelve.'

About to shut the door, he found (as had so many before him) that Mr Harper's person somehow got in the way.

'I've told you, she's out,' he said again.

'I know,' responded Mr Harper. 'Miss Buckley sometimes leaves the rent.'

He did not add that in times past she usually left it with the Duffs.

Ruairi wavered and looked in the direction of the small kitchen — a tactical error, for when he turned again to Mr Harper he found that gentleman had crossed the threshold and was gazing about him with interest.

Ruairi was annoyed. 'Look, I haven't time to be bothered with you,' he said sharply. 'Get out now and come back later.'

Mr Harper paid no heed but strolled to the centre of the large room. Apart from the addition of Mr Mitchell, no changes appeared to have been made.

Meanwhile Ruairi was advancing on him with a threatening countenance. 'Get out will you! You force your way in here . . . '

Mr Harper raised a hand. 'No,' he said, 'I never did. No force. You opened the door. I walked in, that's all. Just tell Miss Buckley next week will be all right. No sweat.'

The younger man said nothing, but stood at the door as Mr Harper moved to depart, and the incident might have closed there had not Annie Duff, mounting the stairs, come face to face with the two men.

Ruairi made a rapid movement to get the door shut, but the lady's sudden rush forward had the effect of stopping Mr Harper in his tracks, so that he remained in the room, frustrating the other's intent.

'So you're putting him out,' Annie observed. 'A very good thing too!'

Before Mr Harper could disclaim any such intention, the subject of this conversation brushed past him (in every sense, for the trailing sheet swished across the floor.) Like a vengeful Agamemnon clutching his robes about him, Ruairi opened hostilities:

'I do not wish to be rude,' he said (and obviously he did) 'but I must insist that you cease to meddle in what is not your concern — you, your sister, and any other old hag in the place!'

He turned abruptly, only to find himself caught up in the sheet and while he freed his trapped foot Annie darted round and placed herself between him and the door.

'Now you listen to me,' she began, her gold-rimmed spectacles slipping a little further down her nose.

'Get out of my way!' he said roughly, actually pushing her, though not with much force.

'Here, hold on there,' the rent collector intervened. 'That's no way to carry on.'

'Thank you, Mr Harper,' responded Miss Duff with vigour, 'but I am quite capable of . . .'

It was at this point, with the three disputants arguing hotly, that Miss Constance Duff chose to descend from the floor above.

In contrast to her sister who was tall and angular, Constance was built on generous lines. Her hair, surprisingly plentiful and still retaining a few black strands, was dressed off her face in the style of 1910. The flesh, now the colour of rich old vellum and pitted here and there with the brown marks of age, was criss-crossed around the ears with tiny fine lines which deepened as she smiled, but in the arch of the brows, the long straight nose and high cheek-bones, could yet be seen traces of the handsome girl she once was.

Holding the banister-rail and taking the steps one at a time, she was descending slowly when Mr Harper spotted her. Now Mr Harper's opinion of Annie could be summed up in the words 'decent old skin', but for Constance he had profound respect, although she would have been considerably surprised had she known of it. He now advanced to help her descend the last few steps, while the quarrel raged behind him.

'Annie,' said the elder Miss Duff, 'whatever is the matter?'

Her sister turned round, surprised into silence, and Ruairi whose normally florid countenance now matched the colour of the blanket, took the opportunity to deliver himself of a few well-chosen epithets.

At these words, the restraints of urban living fell from Mr Harper and his shoulders heaved, but Constance appeared unmoved. She cut in, in her high-pitched voice:

'One day, Mr Mitchell, you will be a great artist, I am sure. And a great artist may be forgiven some things. You are upset. I see you have brought the shopping, Annie. Come, we will go upstairs and give Mr Harper the rent.'

Annie began at once to look for her purse, but Mr Harper (whose sudden rush of blood had subsided) was grateful for the intervention and said he was on his way up in any case.

'Is Miss Brown in?' he asked.

'Someone looking for me?' Janet's dark head hung over the rail above, and Mr Harper, determined to have no more to do with the Mitchell affair, replied cheerfully that he was 'just coming'.

Agamemnon, seeing the forces of Troy in retreat, and becoming for the first time rather self-conscious about his attire, turned and made to do likewise when he was halted by the strong accents of Frances Loughnane mounting the stairs behind him.

'What on earth is going on around

here?' Frances said. 'I could hear the voices out in the street.'

Ruairi, giving her a look of frank revulsion, vanished into his room and slammed the door.

'But what is it?' she enquired again, hunching up her shoulders as the door banged.

She followed the two Miss Duffs up the stairs and having scooped up Janet on the landing all five persons made their way into the Duffs' front room, where Annie related (with relish) the whole of what had taken place.

'Say, he really is some bad guy!' was Janet's comment, when Annie had described how she was pushed and the (unrepeatable) language used.

'It's a downright shame,' muttered Frances. 'Look here Mr Harper, can't you do something? I mean, we didn't raise any fuss about the Kellys moving in, because . . . well, anyway we didn't, but now even old Simms has got someone with him.'

'No — really?' Janet gurgled. 'What a day this is! What's she like?'

Mr Harper looked more than surprised, and the Duffs were frankly astonished. Frances seemed to wish she had not spoken.

'It's not that at all,' she said quickly. 'Kathleen Tracey told me this morning. Apparently he's Leo's cousin and he's staying for a few days.'

A deflated silence followed this explanation.

'I wish you could do something,' Frances said again, 'it was bad enough with just Elizabeth; the same bits of music over and over. But now, when she leaves off he starts up, and just as you think *finally* there's going to be a lull, your man with the 'cello arrives and it goes on till two in the morning.'

Mr Harper took out his pen and jotted down a few notes. 'The original complaint,' he said, looking at Constance, 'was on *moral* grounds.'

'I did feel it was a pity,' said that lady. 'She's such a nice girl and they seem very fond of one another. Why should they not marry?'

'What on earth does she see in that character?' put in Frances, adding under her breath: 'Only his mother could love him!'

Constance was pursuing her own thoughts: 'I believe he is working with Professor . . . ah dear, what *is* the man's name — I'm afraid I'm becoming very forgetful these days,' and Constance paused before adding significantly, '*age*, you know,' (she liked telling people she was eighty-seven).

Before she could continue, however, Janet broke in: 'You mean that he is still just a student?'

Here Constance came into her own. 'Oh yes,' she said at once, 'that young man has a long way to go in his career. Later on no doubt he will move to London or to Vienna or Paris to continue with his studies . . . ' Having created a favourable opening for her own reminiscences, Constance was a little put out when Janet cut in:

'I don't know that I'd care to give any lessons to that Ruairi guy — a few cross words and he'd probably throw the violin at you!'

'Not his own,' Constance remarked

firmly. 'Unless I'm much mistaken, that is a very *valuable* instrument.'

Janet regarded her admiringly. 'You sure know a great deal!'

Constance was pleased. 'When I was your age, my dear, I met many artistically gifted people and saw the world just as you are doing now.'

'Well I don't pretend to understand art or that kind of thing; and as for highbrow music it just leaves me cold.' Here Frances made a realistic gesture.

'Ah, but you are one of the active ones of this world, like my sister Annie here, always busy and often with the unpleasant jobs which others — too lazy perhaps or too indifferent — leave undone.'

Any gratification Frances might have felt was eroded by the comparison with Annie, nor did the latter seem entirely pleased.

'Of course I haven't had your opportunities, Constance,' she began in a huff, but at this point Mr Harper created a diversion by getting up and Annie remembering about the rent turned to search for her purse.

'Did you say Mrs Tracey was in?' Harper asked of Frances, when the money was handed over.

'She was, about a half-hour ago.'

'I'll just go up then and hope to catch her.'

'Be up in a minute myself,' Frances called out as Harper was leaving. 'Poor old Kathleen,' she added, as the door closed behind him, 'she's always hard-pressed.'

'Doesn't her husband work?' asked Janet.

'No. I don't think he ever did. 'Course he's not what you'd call strong. Weak lungs. And then he had that fall and hurt his back. Though where he fell *from*,' added Frances, *sotto voce*, 'is a bit of a mystery.'

Janet raised her dark eyebrows. 'What do you mean? You think there's something odd about him?'

'Wouldn't be surprised,' Frances nodded grimly. 'Anyhow lately old Simms has been sort of hinting I should keep my stuff under lock and key.'

'A pity he wouldn't think of warning

the rest of us then,' retorted Annie. 'Not but that I'm surprised he even took the trouble to tell one person. I wonder what he found out?' she added speculatively.

'There may not have been anything to it. I mean, it was probably only a suspicion. Simms must have a few contacts, living the way he does, and maybe someone gave him the tip.'

'He did definitely name this — what did you call him — Tracey?'

Frances looked at Janet. 'Yes,' she said, 'he did. But that's just between ourselves. You don't want to spread a thing like that around.'

'Quite right my dear,' Constance agreed, 'and poor Mrs Tracey; as you say, she has a difficult time of it in any case.'

'She does have a job?' persisted Janet.

'Waitress in a late-night cafe,' Frances said. 'Well, look, I can't stay here chatting.' She paused. 'You will keep everything I've said to yourselves, won't you?'

They promised they would.

Outside in Organ Place, Elizabeth Buckley returning from her shopping expedition had run bang into the Kellys emerging from the house *en masse*. Elizabeth would have passed with a nod, but Imelda stopped her.

'I didn't know you were out,' Imelda said, clutching Sarah's hand. 'Donal, don't go out in the road there! Here,' she said, moving closer to Elizabeth and lowering her voice, 'you know old Harper's inside? I heard he and your friend had a bit of a dust-up and Harper's putting him out.'

She observed with satisfaction the effect of this news.

'He can't do that,' Elizabeth's rather pale face suffused with colour.

'Can't he though! You should have heard them at it; burn the ears off you! And then old Annie tried to come between them, only she got hit in the struggle.'

'I don't believe you!' Elizabeth said desperately, but all traces of her sudden colour had vanished. Without another word, she turned and ran into the house.

Imelda went on her way unaware of the sensation she thus missed (to her bitter disappointment).

The house was very quiet as Elizabeth mounted the stairs and opened the door of the flat. Some minutes later however, sounds of an argument were to be heard, an argument in which the tenor part became more and more strident.

In fairness to Ruairi it should be stressed that in the earlier confrontation he had managed to keep a normally erratic and volatile temperament under some control, but Elizabeth's anxiety and tentative questions infuriated him where Harper had failed. In the face of his anger, her protests died away and her own temperament took refuge in tears. His shouts of abuse grew louder; he banged on the furniture (causing a prospective customer in Nevin & Flood to gaze anxiously at the ceiling); he threatened, he railed and finally he screamed out that he hoped he never saw Elizabeth, the Duffs, Mr Harper and several other four-by-three adjectival persons of the house ever again.

By this time, a small knot of the self-same persons were gathered on the landing outside, and leaving Tony Flood to attend to their customer, Denise Nevin came out of the shop and went upstairs.

Here she found Annie and Janet in the company of a stocky dark-haired man, who turned out to be Mr Simms' famous cousin. It had been no part of this gentleman's plan to become involved in the scene, but his progress downstairs was impeded by Annie who clutched at his coat saying (as a particularly loud thump came from the first-floor front room):

'Oh, don't you think we should do something?'

The man listened; then went over to the door. What he heard apparently satisfied him for he came back saying he didn't think there was cause for alarm. Then, about to continue his descent, he came face to face with a breathless Mrs Nevin.

'Whatever is wrong?' she gasped, looking from one to the other.

A series of noises suggestive of presses being slammed interrupted her, and Annie cried out. In a sudden lull, female sobs could be heard, and the dark-haired man (against his better judgment) moved over to the door again and knocked.

But his knock was barely audible, for at that moment the most appalling bang smote their ears and caused the floor to tremble under them. This was later found to have resulted from the upright piano having been brought into forceful contact with the wall.

The door then opened, and Mr Ruairi Mitchell emerged clutching his violin-case and an assortment of articles imperfectly stuffed into a hold-all and some bags. He had no doubt intended to stand at the door and deliver himself of various parting words but, becoming aware of a new audience, he carried his attack out to the landing, shouldering past Mr Simms' cousin who prudently withdrew a few paces.

Over Mr Mitchell's farewell speech a veil had better be drawn. Denise Nevin was white-faced and Annie had to be revived later with cups of tea. Janet on the other hand expressed interest, and the dark-haired man offered no comment.

Still mouthing obscenities, Ruairi finally arrived out in the street, where some recollection apparently took place for he went off in search of a taxi clutching his bundles about him.

7

'Number 266: Irish silver coffee pot made in Dublin in 1783, maker . . . '

As the auctioneer's voice droned on, Denise Nevin consulted her list where number 266 did not appear. Representatives of several long-established antique firms entered the bidding, and a gentleman in the far corner who had already purchased several expensive silver items, seemed poised to put in his bid.

The furniture auction was taking place in a large detached suburban house, and the auctioneer's hammer fell not only on the carefully preserved antique but also on items of less value — the latter category mostly being of interest to Denise.

She now contemplated an inkstand of nineteenth century Sheffield plate, the copper being visible at the edges. Otherwise it appeared to be in perfect condition. Fifty pounds might not be too high a price, and many of those present would not bid. After some consideration, she admitted it was unlikely the Nevin & Flood clientele would appreciate the merits of the inkstand. Instead, she turned her attention to item number 275, for which she knew she would find a ready sale. This comprised a set of six Chippendale style chairs, two with damaged backs and one with a broken leg and stretcher. All were in need of some re-upholstering.

Dispassionately she viewed the other bidders, some of whom had raised the inkstand to thirty-five pounds. There would not be any great interest in the chairs, she decided. Well, forty pounds would be her outside figure. They needed quite a lot of work and although old Simms was good with his hands and would repair the woodwork nicely, she herself would have to pad and re-cover the seats and materials were expensive. All the same, if she were pushed she might perhaps rise to fifty pounds.

It was a pity Tony was so hopeless at carpentry. Now Andrew could turn his hand to anything. Even damaged items. Many a walnut bureau or rosewood cabinet picked up in poor condition had later stood in their shop window inviting admiration. As a French polisher, he had excelled. And then there were the clocks. Denise sighed. She still had one or two, genuine French eighteenth century, which had come into his possession chipped, broken, hands missing. He would painstakingly strip them down, find spare parts, carefully repair the damaged areas and then re-assemble the whole in good working order. She had received some attractive offers for the ones she had left, but somehow it had seemed like parting with Andrew himself to let them go. Now she had returned to live at number 49, she might put one up in her own room, perhaps.

One never could tell what Tony might do. He was a good buyer, that she had to admit, and he could handle certain sales very well too. Andrew had liked him, but Andrew had in many ways been still a boy. As long as he could potter around the things he loved, then he was happy.

And if he made a little money also, enough for them to live on, why he was quite content.

Now Tony wasn't like that. Tony was all for expansion — bigger premises, larger profits, vans to collect and deliver. And she had to admit that she Denise Nevin would have been satisfied to carry on in Andrew's mould, with Leo Simms doing the odd repair job.

Through the haze of past reflections, she became aware of the auctioneer's description of the chairs, and hastily settled herself to business. As she had predicted, they excited little interest and the auctioneer, clearly accustomed to better things, closed with her prematurely at thirty pounds.

Very satisfied with this result, she gave further consideration to her list. One or two items were coming up, and she could afford a bit extra now. There was some early nineteenth century glass. That always looked well, and aroused the customer's interest. And a rose-bowl, with two small matching vases in fine porcelain. Sometimes though, small attractive items fetched rather more than their actual worth, and about the vases she would have to hazard a guess.

Later when she had arranged about collection and payment, she turned her attention to another business matter. Tony was right in one respect. If they were to keep the shop open on a daily basis, then an assistant would have to be found. With Tony away travelling so much, even apart from a regular half-day, she often had to close the shop so she could attend auctions, as she had done just now. When Andrew had been alive, of course . . .

She sighed. It wasn't that she didn't enjoy the work. Quite the contrary. Only Tony made things difficult. After Andrew's death, she had considered selling her share in the business and starting up on her own. But there were legal tangles, and Tony had been furious at the idea of taking a stranger into the partnership. Anyhow, at that time she had felt so bereft, the idea of being completely on her own had little appeal. Whereas now . . .

Now, half the time she didn't know where Tony was or what business he transacted. When he pulled off a lucrative deal, he would talk of it for weeks, but these deals did not take place too often. He would return from a week or two of travelling about the country, always with a number of items purchased; and one or two sometimes fetched very good prices indeed. But somehow, she never felt she could depend . . . Perhaps it was because Andrew had been so very dependable. Hardly fair perhaps to expect that much of Tony . . .

Anyway, when she returned to the shop she would phone an employment agency for an assistant. It was a pity she couldn't have had Janet. Janet didn't need the money, but she might have considered doing a little part-time work as an aid to research. However, the American had now got her European trip mapped out — ten countries in two weeks — and was all set to depart.

This reminded Denise she had promised to make space available for the girl's unwanted luggage. She had better organize a safe corner where it couldn't get knocked about. She was actually thinking of this, when she reached the shop door and turned the key in the lock. The shop had been closed since early morning, and had the chill peculiar to old basements. Already it was quite dusk, and before closing the door she went to put on the light.

It is possible this action saved her life.

Even as she depressed the switch, she was conscious of the man's figure. In a sudden split second she saw the masked features and the knife in his hand. Her scream died away in her throat. He was closing with her. Desperately, she threw herself to one side. She felt nothing, but almost immediately there was blood on her sleeve. She could hear his hoarse breathing, as she fought to get away. The furniture hampered him, but she was shut in tight to the wall and a table cut off her retreat. He lunged forward, the knife now edged with red. Her thirty-year-old reflexes were not normally fast, but she flung herself under the table hitting her head and bruising her shins on the brass fender stored underneath. The table was blocked at one end by a bookcase and as she struggled to rise up the other side, she could hear him tugging and pulling at the furniture.

'But the light is on,' she thought, 'someone will see!'

The same thought must have occurred to the man, for he bent down, keeping out of vision of the wide shop window. Denise's hands, groping on the floor, came in contact with several brass objects. Loosely tied up with coarse twine, they consisted of shovel, poker and tongs; all with heavy brass knobs.

She could not get the twine off, and took the whole bundle into her hands. The shovel hampered her and she tugged at the bundle as the seconds raced by. The bookcase was being pulled away; he was nearly upon her. Frantically she tore at the twine and the bundle fell apart, leaving one instrument in her hands. It was the tongs. There was no time. His face breathed into hers, the knife poised to strike. With all her strength, she lunged forward with the heavy end of the tongs, catching him in the chest.

She was half-sprawled under the table,

her legs still caught up in the fender, and in spite of the weight of the tongs the blow had little force. He was winded though, and the knife did not find its mark. Instead, his hand fell forward, burying the knife-point in the floor.

And in that moment, there came shouts and the sounds of hurrying feet. The man ran towards the back of the shop, blundering into furniture which impeded his progress.

Denise lay under the table; weak with relief — still holding the tongs.

Through the open door came a small black furry shape pursued by the eager clutching hands of Sarah Kelly.

'Pompon! Come back.'

The cat vanished into the darkness of the storeroom, and Sarah made to dash in after it.

'No, no,' Denise cried out involuntarily. Perhaps the man had taken refuge there. 'Sarah!' she called urgently, 'don't go in there.'

At the sound of her voice, Sarah turned and gazed around in wonder.

'Over here,' called Denise. The man

might see the child and come back.

Sarah began to peer under the table, delighted with the promise of a game.

'I see you!' she announced triumphantly.

Denise did her best to keep the panic out of her voice, but at that moment the door was pushed right open and the child's mother came in, in a flurry.

'Sarah! Where are you? When I get my hands on that child, I won't be responsible . . . Oh, Mrs Nevin, how you startled me! Is Sarah here?'

At the sound of her mother's voice, Sarah discreetly faded into the background. Denise extricated herself from underneath the table, and advanced towards Imelda. She was shaking all over.

'Thank God you've come,' she said weakly, the tears beginning to spill down her face. She put her arms round the other woman and clung to her.

'Why, whatever is it?' Imelda asked, amazed. 'Are you all right?' And then, becoming aware of the blood staining the heavy coat, she disengaged herself and stood back.

'Sarah!' she cried out. 'Is Sarah hurt?'

Denise tried to fight back the tears. 'Sarah's fine,' she said. 'She's here — come out love and let your Mammy see you.'

Rather shyly, the child emerged from behind a bureau.

'Oh, there you are!' Imelda's voice held relief. 'But what happened?' she asked again.

'There was a man here — he went out the back, I think. He had a knife.' Denise looked at her coat sleeve, where the blood was beginning to crust.

Imelda threw a horrified glance at the entrance to the storeroom. 'Could you walk up the steps?' she asked quickly. 'Better get outside, anyway. Sarah, hold my hand. I'll get my Dad,' she added, 'he'll know what to do.'

Together they left the shop and went up the steps, Denise leaning on the rail for support. She was beginning to feel faint. Joe Gallagher met the procession as it straggled through the front door, and Sarah ran past her mother and went to hold Joe's hand.

'Lady's cryin',' she observed.

'Why Mrs Nevin, what is it?'

'She's been stabbed,' replied his daughter, never one to mince words, 'and we might all have been murdered. Better get a doctor as quick as you can; she's bleeding terrible. And the police too,' Imelda added, as she and her father helped Denise into a chair by the fire.

Joe Gallagher wasted no time, but ran out to the coinbox phone in the hall. When he returned, it was to find his daughter trying to help Denise out of her coat.

'Better leave that,' he said, 'till the doctor comes. I got on to O'Toole down the road; he was at his tea. He said he'll be up in a few minutes.'

Denise lay back in the chair, her face very white. 'You don't know how grateful I am,' she said faintly. 'And if it hadn't been for you that other time as well . . .'

She trailed away, and Imelda looked up into her father's anxious face.

'There!' she cried triumphantly. 'Didn't we say it was all part of the same thing. Someone's out to kill Mrs Nevin!'

8

The following morning, Mr Simms, bowling along the Rathmines Road his handcart piled high with furniture, was reflecting on the events of the previous evening. His road lay downhill and he handled the cart with the ease of long practice, his thoughts almost wholly fixed on the recent happenings at number 49.

The police had come of course; the very sergeant who had interviewed Joe Gallagher at the station and another younger man. They spent some time in the shop and examined the storeroom and the back door leading to a long-neglected garden, where a sad tree grew in a wilderness of nettles and dandelions. It was dark when they arrived and they did not stay long in the garden. What clues the shop and storeroom yielded, if any, they kept to themselves, but the knife of course had remained stuck point downwards in the shop floor, where the intruder's hand had fallen, and this principal exhibit had been taken away.

Mrs Nevin, attended by Dr O'Toole, was found to have a stab wound in the upper part of her left arm. As she steadfastly refused to be taken to hospital (yet again) the doctor had given a local anaesthetic and then stitched up the wound. It was not too serious, he said, but there was the danger of infection. He would give an injection.

Miss Frances Loughnane, returning from a hard day's work, had been so wrought by the news that she straightway announced her intention of staying with Denise, and knocked on Mr Simms' door to ask if he and his cousin would carry down her divan bed. Leo of course was well used to this sort of activity, but the cousin was less dexterous, and as they heaved and pushed, first with the base and then the mattress, they had to listen to a running commentary from Miss Loughnane, who followed with her arms full of bedding.

'Things are certainly hotting up around here,' she remarked, hugging to herself two pillows and a duvet.

'They are,' agreed Mr Simms, as for the second time his cousin got a castor stuck in the stair-rail. 'Hold it away from the wall,' he instructed as the other man wrenching the leg of the base from between the rails then veered away in the opposite direction.

'I'm afraid I'm putting you to a lot of trouble,' said Frances with an air of apology, to which neither man responded.

Two storeys further down, gratefully they toted their burden into the patient's room. No sounds of piano practice came from the first-floor front; indeed the piano had been silent since the preceding Saturday, whether through injury to itself or to the pianist, no one knew.

Having been ordered into bed by the doctor, Denise viewed these arrivals through a drug-induced haze. Her arm did not pain her just now. She felt rather light-hearted. She even remembered to tell Leo about the chairs.

'That's all right, Mrs Nevin,' he replied. 'Give me the address and I will collect them tomorrow. Don't bother about anything now. Mr Flood will see to what needs doing.'

'He's away,' Denise said. 'He went off yesterday.'

'Well, he will soon be back I expect,' was the soothing response.

The cousin, mopping a perspiring brow (despite the cold of a raw November night) nudged Leo at that point and the two men mounted the stairs again to fetch the mattress.

After Sergeant O'Keeffe had completed his investigations below, he then had a further talk with the victim. Frances was present at this interview and afterwards Mr Simms (and cousin) heard what had taken place.

Mrs Nevin was, in the Sergeant's view 'a pretty nice woman'. In her dazed condition, she found it hard to give clear answers to his questions, but he persevered:

'Can you tell us anything at all about your assailant; was he a big man, for instance?'

'Oh no; at least its hard to say really. Most of the time he was stooping. But he was thin, I think.'

'Did you see his face?'

'He wore a stocking pulled over his head.' Denise shuddered. 'His face looked terrible. He had a knitted woollen cap covering his hair.'

'What colour was the cap?'

'Grey I think, or brown. I couldn't be sure.'

'Did you see any hair at all?'

'No.'

'He didn't remind you of anyone you know?'

'What a question!' put in Frances, never silent for long, and Denise lying back on the pillows had a strained look.

She said: 'I'm sorry. I was so terrified. Just blind panic. I'm afraid I couldn't recognize . . . '

'I know,' the Sergeant's voice was soothing. 'Now earlier I think you told me that when the man came at you under the table, you hit out at him with heavy brass fire-tongs. Is that right?'

'I grabbed what was nearest to hand and the tongs just happened to be there. Otherwise . . . '

'Of course. Now if you'll identify the article in question for us, before we take it away.' O'Keeffe got up and went over to the door. His colleague was apparently waiting outside. In a moment the Sergeant came back with a parcel. He pulled aside the wrappings.

'Is this the one you used?'

'Oh yes. As a matter of fact we haven't another like it in the shop.'

'Very good. There is one other thing; your partner, Mr Flood, he was away today?'

'He travels around the country on business.'

'Do you have his itinerary?'

Denise raised herself on her right arm. 'It's not like that,' she said. 'Ours is just a small firm. He attends one or two country auctions, but he often gets word of a private sale where there might be something interesting.'

The Sergeant looked at Frances. Her presence hampered him. However she appeared to be established for the night, so he went on to the next point.

'Now, in the previous assault which

took place outside the shop door, did you get the impression the man there was trying to rob you, or what?'

'The only impression I had was much the same as today,' replied Denise with the ghost of a smile. 'I was terrified.'

'Could it have been the same man?'

'I've really no idea. The man was behind me and when I turned around he rushed at me and forced me down the steps to the shop door, and all the time he kept hitting me on the head, only my parcels got in the way,' Denise paused for breath.

'A tall man, was he?'

'It's hard to say. I'm not very tall, you see. But then I was down at the bottom of the steps in a heap and he was standing over me. It was dark. That's all I know.'

'What *I* want to know,' Frances butted in, 'is what's being done to see Mrs Nevin is not attacked again. This makes three times in as many weeks.'

Sergeant O'Keeffe looked surprised. 'What's this about a third attack?'

'Oh no,' smiled Denise, but with a curious look at Frances. 'It was an accident — a traffic accident.'

The Sergeant turned over a fresh page of his notebook and wrote a new heading. 'I'd like to hear the details please,' he said grimly.

Denise regarded Frances in some vexation, but that energetic girl only made a face. 'It's all over the house,' she said, answering the other's thought. 'We can put two-and-two together, even if you can't.'

The Sergeant was quick to interrupt. 'Let Mrs Nevin start at the beginning. When did this happen?'

'I don't remember exactly,' Denise replied, 'but when I was attacked outside the shop I was returning from the hospital then, and I'd been in for about a week.'

'You mean you were in hospital as a result of being injured in this traffic accident?'

'Yes.'

'Can you tell me what occurred?'

Denise considered, and then went on in a rather tired voice: 'It happened in just a few seconds. I stepped off the path and although I certainly had the *impression* the road was clear, a car fairly whizzed around the corner. It was the sudden noise which alerted me, and I jumped back. But the side of the car hit against my face and body. It gave me a nasty bang on the head and my wrist was fractured.'

'Did you get a look at the driver?'

'Well, it was a man — that I did see.'

'Could you describe him? Would you recognize him again?'

Denise shook her head. 'I don't think so. You see, one minute I was about to cross the road, and the next thing I knew I was lying on my back and people were coming from all directions.' She turned to the Sergeant: 'One witness did get the number of the car, but it turned out to have been stolen.'

Denise gave a little giggle, and the Sergeant regarded her in some concern.

'Yes,' she said, between spasms of laughter, 'you'll get it all in the f..files.'

'Please, Mrs Nevin,' responded the Sergeant, as the patient once more dissolved into helpless laughter, 'please, this is very serious.'

At the last word, Denise fairly howled and even the Sergeant's rather wooden expression softened.

'We have to . . . ' he began.

'I know, I know,' Denise said weakly. 'I'm sorry. It's shock, I think. Don't mind me. I'll be all right in a little while.'

The Sergeant looked at her keenly and decided he had better keep to the matter in hand.

'If you could just go back for a moment to the brass tongs,' he said. 'When you hit out at the man, did he cry out or give a grunt of pain or say anything?'

Denise paused and considered: 'He gave a sort of gasp,' she answered finally. 'I don't think he said anything.'

'You mean,' put in Frances, 'he could now have a bruise where she hit him?'

'Very likely,' replied the Sergeant. Turning to Denise, he asked: 'Was the man wearing an overcoat or jacket?'

'No, he had a polo-neck sweater I think — green or dark-grey perhaps. The ends of the stocking mask were pushed down under the neck of the sweater. He had rubber gloves too.'

The Sergeant, busily writing, finally looked up. 'I wanted to ask you about the child, Sarah Kelly,' he said. 'Could she have got a glimpse of this man, do you think?'

'She didn't see anything,' Denise answered quickly. 'He ran to the back of the shop when he heard her footsteps, and he was gone before she ever came in. My whole *fear*,' and Denise clutched the bedclothes as she spoke, 'I was afraid the man would see it was only a child and come back. But he didn't. And then Imelda came.'

The Sergeant nodded. 'That's very clear,' he said.

'Mind you,' Denise added, relaxing and giving him a smile, 'it's a pity you can't question Pompon. She followed him into the storeroom.'

'Pompon?'

'That's the Duffs' cat,' explained Frances. 'Sarah Kelly was chasing it when it ran into the shop with her after it.'

'I believe we did come across the animal,' the Sergeant responded, inspecting a scratch on the back of his hand. He got up saying he thought the police had enough information for the present.

'But what happens when you've gone,' Frances demanded. 'Supposing your man with the knife comes back tonight?'

'That's hardly likely.'

'Easy for you to say. We have to sleep here.'

'I shouldn't worry. Mr Gallagher below has promised to bolt the front door when we go out now. Anyone coming in later on will have to identify themselves to him, so he says.'

'Joe Gallagher is sixty years of age,' Frances said contemptuously. 'What chance has he against a young man armed with a knife?'

'I don't think the man was that young,' Denise interrupted her, and the Sergeant opened his notebook again. She turned to him: 'It's just an impression I got. I'd say he was thirtyish — not a teenager anyway.'

'That's very helpful, Mrs Nevin. We'll be able to build up a picture.'

'It's a pity we haven't a gun,' Frances said wistfully, and the Sergeant with a prudent man's unease at the thought of weapons in the hands of females, shook his head smiling.

'Just leave this to us, now. There's no cause for alarm.'

'Sez you!' muttered Frances under her breath, as the two policemen went away.

Denise said drowsily: 'Don't let's have any visitors now, will you? I could sleep for a week.'

While complying with this request, Frances nevertheless managed to interview quite a number of people who called to enquire how the patient did; by the simple expedient of conducting conversations on the landing outside. As few of these well-wishers came empty-handed, she was kept busy taking in various articles for the patient's comfort or amusement.

There were magazines from Imelda and a curious little pot of ointment from her father (in case the patient's arm should swell) accompanied by Joe's warranty that 'he had had it for years, in fact it had come to him from his mother, who used to make it!' After one sniff, Frances put it away: she hoped the patient's condition would not become that desperate.

Annie Duff brought nourishing soup made by herself, and a very beautiful lacy wool shawl donated by Constance. Leo arrived holding a bed-rest specially fetched from his place of business. Frances, trying to visualize it transformed by soap and water, agreed it would prove very useful.

Persons arriving home late and reluctantly admitted by Mr Gallagher, were held captive while he imparted the gory details. The first of these turned out to be Janet, who hurried up to the patient's room.

'Frances!' she exclaimed. 'Mrs Nevin — is she badly hurt? I've just heard — it's awful.'

While Frances replied to these enquiries, she wondered if the American intended to share in the nursing. She could do with a bit of support, and if there were a maniac running around with a knife . . . On the other hand, her role carried with it a certain prestige, and if the police were really sure there was no danger . . .

Footsteps sounded on the stairs and Kathleen Tracey came down on her way out to work. Seeing the two girls she paused awkwardly, and Janet said:

'I'll get my things off. Be right back with you!'

She nodded to Kathleen, and tripped lightly upstairs.

Kathleen Tracey was a plain woman in every sense. Aged about forty, she was of medium height, her skin tightly drawn over a large and protruding bone structure. Always neatly dressed, it was difficult to guess at her thoughts and feelings, for she gave no outward sign of having any! And as she made a conventional enquiry about the patient's condition, she seemed to use only a well-worn formula.

Frances would have dealt with her summarily, but the curious fact about Kathleen was that although she seldom spoke to anyone for longer than two minutes, she always seemed to have the latest information! Even now, while putting forward a conventional offer of help, Kathleen added: 'It's a pity Miss

Buckley is away.'

'Away?' Frances looked across the landing to the front room's closed door.

'She hasn't been here for two days.'

'There's been complete silence all right,' Frances said slowly, 'but I thought perhaps . . . '

But Kathleen appeared disinterested in speculation. She tucked her handbag a little further up on her arm. 'I'd better be going,' she said, 'or I'll be late.'

'Oh sure,' Frances responded mechanically, her gaze still riveted on the other door.

This little episode had its sequel.

9

The house had been quiet for some time. Most of its occupants were asleep. Mr Simms (once more in his own bed) snored contentedly. Constance Duff had risen to make herself a cup of tea and to put more coal on the fire, for the night was a bitterly cold one. In the adjoining room, Janet Brown having spent some hectic hours making last-minute plans for her departure had finally tumbled into bed.

In the room below, Denise Nevin lay awake. It was rotten to be ill, and she had been so much in pain lately. Even more rotten to think someone wanted to kill you. Who could want to do that? It wasn't as if her death benefited anyone. Unless Tony. She pushed that thought away. The man in the shop wasn't Tony. Tony was somehow bigger — broader. She wished and not for the first time, that she need not be alone. How nice for Imelda Kelly to have the three kids with her, and her father within call. Even if the husband *had* gone off . . .

Well, there it was. She herself had had six happy years with Andrew. They had not been very exciting years but she had been happy. And if it was a pity they'd had no family, it hadn't bothered her too much then. Now Andrew was dead and there was no one. He had two sisters but they were married and remote from her.

She looked across the room to where Frances lay flat on her back and immobile. Frances was tired out and it would be a shame to wake her, but Denise did wish she could have a drink. There was a glass of lemon at her elbow, but she longed for a cup of tea. Oh well, the lemon drink would quench her thirst, and better to be here than among strangers.

She hoped Joe Gallagher had remembered to bolt the front door. He had said he would. Still, people had to be free to come and go, and Joe couldn't stay up all night. Her own door was locked too, and from the picture rail above, Frances had suspended two rubber hot-water bottles designed to drench the unwary intruder (a more complex arrangement had been made to defend the window).

People were very kind, when all came to all. She wondered what would happen on the morrow. Frances had to be up early to go to work, and the Duffs had promised to stay with her during the day, but they were so old and anyway one couldn't . . . As Kathleen Tracey had said, it was a pity Elizabeth Buckley . . .

And at that point, the patient remembered no more but drifted away into restless slumbers.

It was approximately 4 a.m. Outside in the street, Vincent Molesworth had been ringing the bell, on and off, for about fifteen minutes. Not entirely sober, and conscious of a longing for the prone position, his normally kindly nature restrained him from attacking the door with too much vehemence, while at the same time instincts of self-preservation urged him not to linger in the sub-zero temperature of the street. He was therefore turning over in his mind the various alternatives open to him at that hour when another man came down the street, and began to mount the steps behind him.

Mr Molesworth turned rather abruptly. He was a tall man, with a certain elegance of speech not unsuited to his profession.

'These are hard times,' he enunciated clearly, 'who are you, friend?'

'Don't be an idiot!' came the sharp reply. 'It's me — Ruairi.'

Vincent laughed. 'The famous — not to say infamous — Mr Mitchell. I congratulate you! To return to these premises at all requires a certain insensitivity. To endeavour to gain admittance at four o'clock in the morning is to display a total disregard for the opinions of one's fellow-man.'

Ruairi paid no attention to the beginning of this speech, merely seizing on the point of interest.

'Is the door shut, then?'

'Shut, bolted and barricaded against all comers.'

'Have you tried the key?'

Vincent looked pained. 'I may be a *trifle* . . . ' he began, but Ruairi brushed past him and inserted his own key in the lock. The door would not budge.

Before the actor could stop him, he had raised the heavy iron knocker and thundered on the door, at the same time pressing his finger on the bell.

'My dear fellow, do stop that,' Vincent murmured anxiously, 'we don't want to rouse the whole house.'

'They can all get out of bed, for all I care,' retorted Ruairi, jabbing again at the bell.

In the adjoining window, the heavy lace curtains were pulled aside and the figure of Joe Gallagher appeared, clad in flannelette pyjamas. Mr Molesworth prudently effaced himself while the young musician angrily demanded to be let in.

At first it seemed as if he was going to be successful, for Joe disappeared from the window and they could hear the inner door open, as he came out into the hall.

However, all that happened was that the letter-box slit was pulled back, and a nose and eye came into view. Inside, a voice was heard to say that the door would not be opened to Mr Mitchell at that or at any other hour and should there be further disturbance, the police would be summoned, good night.

The letter-box shut with a snap, and they could hear the inner door close again.

Ruairi muttered savagely, and gave the door a kick.

'Now see what you've done,' Vincent said plaintively, vistas of his snug warm bed fast diminishing.

'Well, you didn't get very far yourself!'

'Hasty words, hasty words. While my blood has been slowly congealing on these steps, I have resolved to put into practice a well-accustomed exercise, in which you dear sir shall assist me; your head being (from the look of you) rather clearer than mine.'

'What are you talking about?'

'Number fifty, dear fellow, or in words of one syllable the house-next-door.' As he was speaking, he moved to his left and began fumbling in his pockets. The door of number 50 was beside that of number

49 and the broad granite steps ran the whole way across with no railing or other division between.

Ruairi watched speculatively, while the other man slowly turned out his pockets, to be eventually rewarded by the tinkle of a key falling at his feet. Vincent bent down and felt about with his hands, finally kneeling on the steps and gazing around in perplexity.

'Here,' said Ruairi, abruptly coming over and picking up the key. He pushed it into the actor's outstretched hand.

Mr Molesworth got to his feet, staggering a little. However he recovered himself, gazed solemnly at the brass item in his hand, pointed it the right way round and then advanced on the keyhole as though playing darts. He had turned the key and was actually in the hallway of number 50, when Ruairi caught him up.

'What are you doing?' the violinist whispered urgently.

'Going to bed,' responded Mr Molesworth. He pointed up the stairs. 'Have to go to the top.'

Ruairi carefully shut the door behind

them. 'I didn't know there was a way through.'

The other man simply nodded and went to the foot of the stairs. 'Don't make a row; caretaker's in the basement.'

'Where did you get the key?' asked Ruairi, but Mr Molesworth merely put an uncertain finger to his lips and began to climb.

The hall of number 50 differed from that of number 49. For a start, the floor-covering was highly polished and exuded a pleasant aroma. There were thick buff mats across the entrance and at the inner doors. These doors were painted white as was stair and banister. Even in the gloom, the solid brass banister-rail gleamed. And, coming from the freezing cold outside, the two men were at once conscious of the warm air around them.

In silence, they mounted to the first-floor landing, with standards of heat and decoration similar to those of the hall below. On the top landing, they paused for breath. Ruairi looked at the office rooms, whose doors were shut.

'Where now?' he asked.

His companion said nothing, but still pointed upwards. The door of the attic room (the opposite number to his own in 49) was slightly ajar, and he went up the stairs and pushed it open. It gave easily, and he went inside and switched on the light. The room housed cardboard packing-cases and odds and ends of office furniture: a desk with some wooden chairs piled on top, a rolled-up strip of worn carpet, several battered typewriters and a solid old-fashioned press with sliding glass panels. There were, in addition, the usual heaps of dusty files and index cards.

Ruairi looked for a door in the far wall which he imagined might connect with the next house, but there was none. His companion meanwhile made his way across the room, carefully stepping between packing-cases. He removed the pile of chairs from the top of the desk and gently drew the desk towards him. It grated on the bare wooden boards. Mounting it, he began to push at the skylight above.

'Some time since I came this way,' he mumbled. 'Seems to be . . . wait a bit . . .'

'What are you doing?' Ruairi asked.

'Trying to open the window,' came the rejoinder. 'Ah, here it comes. Bit rusty. Well, now. I'll go first. Put out the light and I'll give you a hand up — OK?'

'You mean,' Ruairi enquired flatly, 'we are going out on the roof?'

' 'Course, old son. What do you think I meant?' Vincent gave a final heave to the skylight and laid it back against the roof while he clambered through. Then he reached down an encouraging arm and adjured the other to 'come on now and mind the loose slate.'

Ruairi stepped up on the desk and poked his head through the open window. The cold black night met his face, and he demurred.

'I can't see a thing,' he said. 'Suppose one of us slips. We could fall off.'

'Fall off?' Vincent repeated querulously. 'Fall off where? This is the valley. Roof front and back. 'Course,' he added with apparent willingness to set things in a just light, 'you go down to the end there and you'll fall off!'

'I believe you,' Ruairi responded grimly, as he clambered through the opening, shielding his left hand. He slid downwards (avoiding the loose slate pointed out by Mr Molesworth) and was able to brace his feet on the rising slope of the front roof.

He could hear Vincent close down the skylight, tugging at the rusty iron hasp, accompanied by a muttered:

'Don't suppose it matters if it's not shut tight. Pane of glass's broken anyway.'

Ruairi did not move but waited for the other to come alongside him. Then he said: 'You go ahead. I'll follow.'

'Sure thing,' responded the actor, and led the way forward a trifle unsteadily.

They came to a small obstruction, and Vincent climbed out of the valley and up the side of the sloping roof, carefully descending again the other side.

'Mind, there's glass here,' he warned his companion, 'window's lower down.'

He found the latch and raised it up, allowing Ruairi to scramble through with a murmured 'step on the cooker.'

Ruairi sat on the edge of the roof and discovered that his feet did indeed come to rest on a solid foundation. Gratefully, he descended from the cooker and watched the actor follow suit.

'There now,' said Vincent, 'no bother, eh?'

A little later, the key of the first-floor front room turned noiselessly in the lock and Ruairi stepped in gently. Darkness shrouded the room but in one corner light from the street lamp outside threw the pattern of the curtain in a leering grinning face against the wall, and by this light Ruairi managed to steer a course clear of the kitchen table and presses.

There came a slight movement from the bed and Ruairi turned and whispered urgently: 'Don't start screaming or anything — it's me.'

Getting no response, he peered forward. 'You awake?' he said.

Again, there was no answer and he continued more sharply: 'Elizabeth — it's Ruairi.'

'So what!' came in muffled tones from

the depths of the bed.

'Now look here . . . ' he came forward abruptly, then stopped. 'About the other day . . . you didn't take it seriously? It's not important. What's important is Friday's concert, and today's Tuesday.'

The form in the bed heaved convulsively and Ruairi cried out angrily: 'Shut up, you little fool!'

He came and sat at the end of the bed. 'Look, don't be more stupid than you can help and for a start quit bawling. What are you crying for? There's nothing to cry about.' A short pause, and then he continued: 'Anyway, that's what I came to tell you. I'm moving back in.'

A sound somewhere between a wail and a snort came from underneath the clothes. There was another sound also but Ruairi apparently did not hear it, for he went on a shade more defiantly:

'Look . . . take it easy, will you. I mean, everything between us can be . . . you know . . . the way it was.'

'Hardly, I feel,' said a cool voice close to him and at that moment strong arms held him in their grip.

128

'Put on the light, would you?' continued the voice, as the occupant of the bed rose up to reveal good height and weight, and went to do as he was bid.

When the lights came on, Ruairi vainly struggling with his captor was surprised into sudden quiescence.

10

The ship plunged about in a choppy sea. A small freighter, she hardly seemed a match for the Atlantic waves energetically pushing and churning. Little white waves everywhere. On a narrow bench, a man sat close to the door of the engine room. A damp heat warmed his back while he gazed out on the grey vista. The wind — force five — blew a steady northeast by north and visibility was around three miles.

The discomforts of his new-found freedom differed but little from those of his imprisonment. He was still cold, dirty, and badly fed. That is, the food on this creaking old tub, adequate enough for hardened stomachs, was difficult for an old man to keep down.

He shared a cabin with five other men. Above the engine room, it had a temperature of 90° at all hours. It had artificial light but ventilation only from the door, left open weather permitting. His bunk contained a fibre mattress and thick grey blankets, all smelling of long unbroken use. He was glad to be alive.

Huddled in a sheltered corner of the ship's after-deck, he reflected on events just past. *He had got away with it.* Over and over, he hugged that knowledge to himself. The sensation of sheer excitement, the pounding heart-beat when he had come on board, the surge up of exaltation when the ship had pulled away out into the murky waters, knowing that he, Michael Doyle, had survived where a younger stronger man might easily have gone under. Oh yes, that had made the blood pulsate, and thirty years spent in business deals and urban society was wiped away in one sheer primitive moment.

Now he would have to make a plan. To a man of his experience, that should present little difficulty. Already the voyage was three days' old. He had choice of several ports, or he could stay on board. He would be safer on the ship, but security was no longer his prime consideration. Get Whelan — that was it.

From being a hunted animal, the determination was growing within him to become instead the pursuer. They had planned to be rid of him. Well, they had failed. Now it was his turn. Put Whelan away — fifteen, maybe twenty years. And that *bitch* . . . An old man's folly had it been? He used not to think so. He had been blind, *blind*. But in the early years, she had been winsome; so light-hearted and loving. It was like having his youth again, the youth he didn't have because he was poor and he worked and worked to be rich. And Kate? She had seen it all, hadn't she? Elegant, ambitious Kate with her beautiful clothes and her dry sardonic humour. She had parted from him without a word said in anger almost — simply pocketed his generous allowance and taken herself off to cosmopolitan haunts where she existed elegantly and luxuriously. No men either. Well, none that he'd heard of. Kate was . . . well, Kate.

And then there was Bernie. His heart beat faster when he thought to himself how Whelan must have felt when he heard about Bernie. That had been the start of his fight back — his trump card. What a pity he hadn't been there to see their faces. Possibly they hadn't believed it at first. But he felt sure they had checked. Couldn't afford not to. Two million was at stake — nearer three. And checking took time. So they had held off for a bit, and that had given him his chance to escape.

No doubt they hadn't yet grasped the full extent of his awareness of the plot. How could they? On that last day, he had given no sign, nothing but the one piece of information left for them to find. Yet he had known for weeks prior to that, and only the discovery of his own immediate danger had brought about his hasty, and as it turned out, successful exit.

It just showed how a man like Whelan could be fooled.

The thing was, what should be done now? In spite of his success there remained a nagging anxiety which he could not shake off. He reasoned it away, but again it returned.

If he was to hunt Whelan down, he must go to the police. From a position of security he must convince them of the truth of the danger in which he stood. Then perhaps those uneasy cold fingers which gripped at his heart would disappear.

For a long time he sat there thinking, the grey fretted sea a backdrop to his sombre thoughts. In the end, he arrived at his inevitable decision.

11

'How is the case coming along?' the pretty secretary enquired.

'Well, we do at last seem to have a case,' the Inspector responded, sprawling in his well-worn office chair.

Miss Sheila Curran removed two coffee cups from the litter of loose papers and files on the desk. More files lay in untidy heaps on the floor.

'What's Mrs Nevin like?' she asked.

Detective Inspector Moss Coen pulled at his dark hair and ran his stubby fingers through it. 'There you have me, Sheila,' he answered. 'On the surface, she appears to be a perfectly ordinary fairly youngish widow who runs a modest business with her late husband's partner.'

Sheila Curran cocked an enquiring eye, and the Inspector met her glance.

'Oh, we are looking into the affairs of Mr Tony Flood certainly. Only so far we haven't come up with anything. He is fairly well known in the trade. He buys regularly, mainly at country auctions and sales. The worst that has been said of him is that he's 'sharp'. He is thought to have a very shrewd idea of the value of what he buys and sells, and does a certain amount of business unconnected with Nevin & Flood. In short, he seems a man who might perhaps fear the *tax* inspector!'

Miss Curran looked doubtful. 'That sounds all right, but . . . '

'Oh I know. We're only at the beginning. Here is a woman in no way remarkable who has had two and possibly three attempts made on her life, and all she can say is that there could be no reason for them! No one, she says, could benefit by her death. That, of course, is not strictly true. Tony Flood *would* benefit, but probably only to a small extent. These partnership things are a bit difficult to disentangle. We'll have to dig up a certain amount of information — when exactly Andrew Nevin died, and what provisions were made by him, if any.'

Sheila Curran wrote busily in her

notebook. Then she looked up. 'What about the other people in the house — rather a lot of them, aren't there? What about them?'

'It's like a rabbit-warren,' Moss said feelingly.

There was silence for a moment, and then his secretary said: 'When you went to stay there, did you . . . I mean, was it because of this case?'

Moss got up and paced around the room. 'It was and it wasn't,' he said. 'When the first report came in, it seemed to be a fairly routine case. There were no clues as to the identity of the attacker, and enquiries failed to establish any motive other than possibly robbery. It was the combination of Mrs Nevin having just left hospital, while her partner Tony Flood was conveniently absent in Nenagh, that raised a query. That and the fact that she had been in hospital at all. I couldn't help wondering *why* . . . But there again, it might have been all quite innocent. Everything we've dug up so far suggests that Flood *is* innocent. Really what it boils down to is that if it hadn't been for the curious coincidence of my cousin Leo actually living in that house, I probably would have left it alone. As it was, I felt I could do a little quiet checking, and no harm done if everything turned out OK.

'Old Leo was rather surprised to see me of course, but he knew at once what I was on to. No flies on Leo.'

'He is really your cousin?'

'Certainly he is — you know him then?'

'I know him to see,' Sheila replied with careful distinction.

Moss gave a short laugh. 'Don't let his appearance put you off. Leo has plenty of the ready. What he's done with it all, nobody knows. There'll be some queer secrets revealed after Leo's laid to rest.'

'Why does he live like that?'

'Seems incredible, doesn't it?'

Miss Curran regarded her boss with an indulgent eye. 'Maybe your cousin is a bit eccentric,' she said.

'Well, we all have our peculiarities,' Moss replied sweepingly, 'and Leo appears to be perfectly happy living in his slum.'

'Organ Place isn't a slum!'

'Well, it's heading in that general direction.'

'Nonsense,' Miss Curran responded with spirit, 'a bit of pulling together and a few coats of paint and that place could be made into what estate agents call 'a prestige location'.'

'Oh, the *location* is all right. Care for a room there?' Moss added slyly, 'I could probably get you one. A Miss . . . ' he consulted his notes. 'Ah yes — a Miss Janet Brown is leaving the day after tomorrow on a grand tour of Europe — back in two weeks' time, but she won't be staying as she is returning to the US.'

'I'll let you know,' Sheila said drily.

'Well don't leave it too long. I mean, such a prestige apartment is bound to be snapped up . . . '

She interrupted him: 'Is that the room where you arrested Ruairi Mitchell?'

'My dear girl, we haven't arrested Ruairi! We could, I suppose, bring a charge of unlawful entry or of behaviour likely to lead to a breach of the peace, but in fact the story he tells may quite possibly be true — that he had a row with the woman he's been living with and they broke up, only he's been miserable since, or so he says, and also (and more important) she's a member of his string quartet or whatever — no, I remember now she plays the piano — anyhow they have a concert looming on Friday and she's gone missing.'

'*Missing?*'

'It's no use looking at me like that. *I* don't know. What with having to mount a round-the-clock guard on the fair Denise who refuses to go to hospital — not saying it isn't easier to guard her where she is. But we can't keep that up for very long, and as soon as we take our man away, there she is — a target once again. And God only knows but the fellow may kill someone else. As long as we can't figure the motive, where are we?'

'Maybe other people in the house know something; something Mrs Nevin can't tell you. The Duffs seem to have been there for a very long time, and elderly women usually see all that goes on — if they're not senile, that is.'

Moss smiled grimly. Whatever the

Duffs were, senile they were not.

An hour or so later actually saw him accept a cup of tea from the redoubtable Annie. With Annie, one didn't have to put the questions, but merely to avoid interrupting her natural flow of words.

'I knew he was a bad lot,' she was saying, 'coming in here without let or hindrance, and really Elizabeth whom you always said was such a nice girl, Constance, well all I can say is . . . '

Constance interposed: 'I did my best to advise Miss Buckley,' this with a nod to the Inspector, 'but afterwards I felt we should not become further involved.' She gave Annie a warning look, and went on: 'People sometimes resent good advice, especially when their own inclination runs counter to it.'

'What we have had to put up with!' Annie continued, scarcely listening to her sister's words. 'He abused us. He actually hit me. Mr Harper was a witness. Mr Harper is the rent collector, you know.'

'We've met,' said Moss.

'He told you about it, did he?'

'Oh yes,' Moss responded easily, 'he

gave me all the details.'

Annie smiled a grudging smile, and removed some pieces of sewing from the back of the Inspector's chair. The room was littered with various materials and garments in the making.

Moss took the opportunity to settle himself comfortably in the chair, and balance the teacup on his knees, as he broached the subject of his visit: 'As a matter of fact I was hoping you might be able to let me have some information about Mrs Nevin. Until she is feeling a little better, we cannot question her as we would like.'

Annie nodded graciously, and Constance offered no comment although she favoured the Inspector with a penetrating glance. At this point, a high-pitched cry came from the landing outside. Annie got up at once and opened the door. Pompon, with swishing tail and a rather wild look in her unusually big eyes, burst through Annie's legs. She paused, seeing the Inspector, and then gave a sudden spring up on one of the beds.

The room, which contained some of

the Duffs' own furniture, had an air redolent of an age long gone. It seemed to Moss that upwards of twenty photographs, some in silver frames, adorned the walls, the mantelpiece, and also filled any available spaces between bric-à-brac on the two small tables and the elaborately carved sideboard. The carpet, reddish-brown and with a pattern of large dark-brown medallions, had been of good quality but was now worn very thin in places. Nottingham lace curtains, yellow with age, shrouded the window and any light which penetrated was further obscured by dusty brown velvet drapes. In the physical sense, it was not an attractive room but it had its own charisma.

Even Moss could not quite shake off his feeling of stepping into the past as he confronted Constance. Annie was different. You could meet Annie any day of the week. A decent sort, no doubt, but a trial to live with. Now Constance was not like that at all. Constance Duff recalled an age even more remote than her own. There was somehow a picture of talent and exuberant living faintly washed around the edges with hard times and scanty meals. Moss wondered, he wondered very much, how Constance Duff had managed to accustom herself to the milieu of Organ Place.

And indeed, Annie was busy telling him how long ago that was. 'Of course things are not at all the same now as when we first came to live here.'

'Hardly,' was Constance's dry comment.

'Our brother was with us then, you see,' Annie explained to Moss.

'Oh yes?' This is going to be a long session, thought Moss, but he persevered. 'He is now in a home I believe?'

'Imagine your knowing that!' Annie exclaimed, while Constance remarked: 'But in these cases the police must of course check on everybody. However,' she went on with a slow smile, 'I beg you won't begin to suspect our Jack. He's eighty-three and bedridden.'

Moss was quick to deny any such insinuation. 'And please don't think my visit today is in any way a personal one,' he added, fearing they might take offence, and a valuable source of information thereby dry up. 'It is simply that we must try to find out why anyone would want to injure Denise Nevin.'

'Well, as to that,' Annie began, and Moss took heart.

'Yes?' he prompted.

'Perhaps I shouldn't say anything,' Annie continued with an anxious look at Constance.

'Yes?' Moss again urged. Constance said nothing, and Annie took the plunge.

'Her husband, her *late* husband that is, was a very nice man — just a *little* unworldly,' Annie paused for dramatic effect, her goldrimmed spectacles poised as if to slither down her long thin nose.

Constance regarded her sister in evident amusement. 'No doubt the Inspector will have heard all about that from his cousin,' she said. In an earlier part of the interview, the Coen-Simms relationship had already been discussed at length, with predictable exclamations from Annie, and a kind of watchful intelligence on the part of Constance. Moss told himself it was ridiculous to be unnerved by an old woman of eighty-seven (or whatever Miss Duff's real age was) but he did sincerely wish he might have Annie to himself for ten minutes or more.

As usual, Annie paid little attention to her sister's remarks. 'As I was saying,' she went on, 'Andrew Nevin . . . '

' . . . was an idiot!' Constance concluded with a little laugh. Seeing the Inspector's expression, she went on more soberly. 'He lived in his own little world and he made that pretty young girl he married live in it too.'

'And then he brought that flashy fellow, Tony Flood, into the partnership,' Annie chimed in.

'And he died,' said Moss, 'about two years ago, wasn't it?'

'You mustn't think . . . ' Annie began.

'No, no,' Constance said in the same breath. 'His death was perfectly natural. I mean it was sudden, of course, in fact there had to be an inquest . . . '

The Inspector who had the report of the inquest even now sitting on his desk, said: 'Circulatory trouble, wasn't it?'

'Thrombosis,' Annie confirmed, with a quick jerk of the head. 'Never took any exercise, of course.'

'He was overweight?'

'Thin as a rake,' was Annie's short reply. 'But he never set foot outside the shop practically. Worked there all day long. And Tony Flood and Mrs Nevin used to do the buying, like they do now. Only of course, now Mr Flood can do much as he pleases with the business. Denise is no match for the likes of him.'

'That's not to say,' Constance put in at once, 'that the same man would deliberately injure her. I'm sure he would not.'

Moss appeared quite surprised at such a suggestion. 'So it comes to this,' he went on, 'as far as you are aware, no one could have a motive for killing or injuring Mrs Nevin. What about the shop itself? Could it perhaps contain a valuable item, an article whose value might be unsuspected by the owners?'

'I should imagine Mr Flood is well aware of the value of the shop's contents,' Constance replied drily. 'Of course there are always paintings.' She seemed to consider. 'I should not say Tony Flood is an expert in *that* field. Your cousin now,' and she smiled graciously at Moss, 'Leo Simms could probably help you there.'

The cat, which had been quietly seated on the bed, jumped up suddenly and gave a low hiss. A little startled, Moss turned round. Large baleful pale-orange eyes met his and a rumbling sound came from the cat's throat.

'What is it?'

'Oh, don't mind her,' Constance replied. 'At a time like this, she's a little nervous that's all. Probably heard footsteps on the stairs.'

'I believe your cat was on the scene when Mrs Nevin was attacked in the shop,' said Moss. He was not particularly fond of cats, but people who were fond of them were usually eager to talk about their pets, nor was Constance an exception.

She said at once: 'When Andrew Nevin was alive, Pompon took rather a fancy to him — I don't know why. Certainly she has never shown affection towards any *other* human. She used to spend a lot of time with him in the shop, and she probably still has a hide-out down there; you know how animals will not leave a place once they've developed an attachment to it.'

Just then, there came a sharp knock at the door and Pompon sprang perilously from the bed, landing on Constance's knee with nails outstretched.

'Oh you bad cat!' the lady exclaimed, as she with difficulty extracted clinging claws from her grey flannel skirt.

The door opened to admit Joe Gallagher, and Annie rose to her feet.

'I heard the Inspector was here,' Joe began. 'You're wanted on the phone, sir, down in the hall. They said it was urgent.'

'Be back with you in just a moment,' Moss nodded apologetically to the two ladies.

But he had to send Joe up again with a message of regret, as he hurried away to the station. The body of a man found the previous day had been taken to the City Morgue. Apart from the more obvious injuries sustained, an autopsy had revealed the existence of a small circular mark or bruise just under the region of the heart.

12

'Any idea who he is?' Moss was asking.

The question was addressed to Sergeant O'Keeffe who had accompanied the Inspector to the morgue. In front of them lay the body of an undernourished-looking man of around fifty. The hair, rather thin and plentifully streaked with grey, lay damp against the white face. The bloodless lips were drawn apart, exposing the teeth, and there was a small growth of dark beard.

'Whoever he is, he saw what was coming to him,' O'Keeffe said. 'Look at his face!'

The Inspector, who heartily wished he didn't have to look, grunted his assent. He then transferred his attention to the body. 'Three stab wounds,' he muttered, and he turned to O'Keeffe and added abruptly: 'What do you make of that?'

Sergeant O'Keeffe was a cautious man. 'The State Pathologist's office will let us have their report later, sir.'

'I know. In the meantime, what do *you* think?'

'Well I'm no doctor, sir, but at least one of those wounds doesn't look to me as though it could cause death. I mean *that* one,' and the Sergeant put out a pointing finger.

'That's what I thought myself,' Moss said. 'So it seems likely this killing wasn't premeditated. An assignation perhaps; some talk, then a quarrel and finally several blows delivered at random until the victim dies. When we find out who he is, we may be able to get a line on his general background, friends etc. What about clothes?'

'At present, they're working on the clothes. We have a list.' O'Keeffe went out of the room, and returned with a sheet of paper which he handed to the Inspector.

'Green shirt, dark-green tie, brown slacks, grey tweed jacket,' Moss read out. 'That's certainly suggestive. Let's have a look at the bruise again.'

The two men moved closer to the body

and Moss gave the discoloured skin close attention.

'How long has this man been dead?'

'Well, they don't know exactly, sir, but apparently about thirty hours. The body was found yesterday afternoon at around 4.20 p.m. The finder was a young German seaman.'

'Oh, and what did he have to say for himself?'

A grin spread over O'Keeffe's normally rather wooden features. 'Quite a good deal — a lot of it in his own language. They had to get an interpreter. Although he spoke good English. But he'd had a bad shock apparently, and kept wandering off into his own tongue. Indeed you couldn't blame him. He was only a lad.'

'His story checks out?'

'There was very little trouble about that. His ship is berthed at Alexandra Basin, and the captain confirms that this seaman — Horst Pressler is his name — went ashore at ten o'clock. Pressler says he spent the day sight-seeing. One of our men on duty at the National Museum, saw him there around 2.30 p.m.

And earlier in the day, a bus conductor remembers Pressler arriving in Beresford Place on a number 53 bus, and asking to be directed to O'Connell Street. From the first medical reports, it seems almost certain that at that time our man was already dead.'

Moss ruffled up his coarse dark hair and then smoothed it down again. 'OK, that's clear enough. Exit Herr Pressler. What else have we got?'

'Not very much, sir. The park keeper says that shortly after the park opened that morning, he walked past the spot were the body was later found. He is positive the body was not there when he was on his rounds, but he remembers a man who came into the park very early and sat near the little shelter. The park keeper said he noticed him because he hadn't seen him before, and at this time of year most of his visitors are regulars. He says he can't be absolutely certain it's our stab victim, but he's prepared to say the two were very much alike.'

'What time was this?'

'Shortly after nine.'

'The man was waiting for someone, he thinks?'

'Yes.'

Moss began to pace up and down. For obvious reasons, the room was unheated. He rubbed his hands together.

'Did the park keeper see anyone speak to this man?'

'Seemingly not. There were only a handful of people in the park at the time. He went on his rounds. When he returned to the shelter, the man had gone.'

'What about this *handful*? Can he describe any of them?'

'Some he knew well by sight: a group of middle-aged cleaning women who come from nearby offices. They walk through the park every morning at that hour. Then there were women with prams, taking children to school, and a number of men and women on their way to work. None of the people he saw looked as if they had come to meet the victim. In fact, it was so cold he didn't think anyone would want to sit around. Even the usual pensioners — a few men with dogs that he mostly knows — even they kept on the move. He

154

says that is why he particularly took note of the man near the shelter; all the time he had him in view the man remained seated.'

'I suppose we should be grateful to this witness,' Moss growled, 'even if the evidence *is* of the negative kind. It looks as if our victim did come to keep an appointment and the party who stabbed him exercised some caution before and after so doing. What about *after*, by the way? There'd be a certain amount of blood flowing. I suppose I needn't ask if the keeper noticed anyone dishevelled and blood-stained rushing headlong from the park?'

The Sergeant grinned. 'He did not,' he said emphatically, 'nothing out of the ordinary all day. The only thing that bothers him is how the body could have lain there unnoticed. He says he must have passed very close to it at least once, but either the trees or the hedge hid it from view.'

'He didn't hear any cry or a shout?'

'*He* didn't, but one of the gardeners heard what might have been a cry, although possibly it was just a seagull. He actually stopped work and listened, but the sound wasn't repeated and apparently there was a gull hovering overhead, in fact there were quite a few of them, so he thought no more about it. The time would be about right though — close on ten o'clock. He remembers because shortly afterwards he went for his morning cup of tea.'

'So no one saw and no one heard? Just our luck! Still, we might get something yet — we can put out an appeal for witnesses. This has been in all the news bulletins, I take it?'

'Late last night, and again early this morning. And in today's newspapers, of course.'

'No one has yet come forward to claim the body? That's rather odd, surely?'

'Sometimes they don't,' said the Sergeant. 'You know, sir, they keep on hoping it isn't Sean or Mary or whoever, even though the description fits. Although they're worried stiff, there is always the chance Sean may still turn up, and if he does, sometimes he wouldn't thank them for having been to the police. When the missing person has been gone for a few days, *then* they come. But it can be as long as even a week or two.'

Moss nodded gloomily. 'Oh I know only too well,' he said. The very blue eyes gazed reflectively at the bare wall. 'Anything on the knife yet?' he added.

'It appears to be very much the same, if not actually identical to the one found at the scene of the attack on Mrs Nevin,' was the Sergeant's formal reply. Unbending slightly, he continued: 'That seems to make the whole thing tie in with the Nevin affair, doesn't it, sir?'

'It does not,' his boss replied irritably. 'If this is the fellow who stabbed Mrs Nevin, as that bruise might lead us to believe, then why should he himself be stabbed, and with a similar knife?'

'Revenge?' the Sergeant suggested hopefully.

Moss glanced at him sharply, but in the end offered no comment. He hunted in his pockets for his pipe, then looked down at the cold figure in front of him and finally muttered something about 'getting on with the job.'

Together the two men left the building and walked around the corner into Store Street, where the Inspector had parked his car. They had left the Custom House behind them and had crossed Butt Bridge, when the Sergeant again spoke:

'You mentioned, sir, about the colour of the man's clothes being suggestive. Why was that?'

Moss's temporary irritation had disappeared. They were in a long stream of traffic moving along City Quay and the car swept forward in the direction of Westland Row.

'Well, you yourself questioned Denise Nevin after her attack. Her impression of the man's clothing — what she could see of it — was that it was either grey or green. That might well be for reasons of camouflage, but if by any chance they were the man's own clothes . . . By a curious coincidence, our stab victim's clothes are also grey and green.'

'You think he's the same man?'

'I don't know *who* he is,' Moss replied with vigour. 'One thing though. We'll show Mrs Nevin a few photographs and watch her reactions.'

The Sergeant had been under the impression they were returning to Organ Place, but the Inspector's car left the narrow city streets behind and headed out towards the suburbs. Finally it came to rest outside a block of well-kept luxury flats. Moss got out and the Sergeant (after some hesitation) followed.

'Where are we, sir?'

Moss looked amused. 'I thought we'd have a little chat with Mr Tony Flood,' he said. 'Does himself well, doesn't he? Why, his share of the profits from Nevin & Flood wouldn't cover the rent of a place like this! That's where these lads make their mistake. As soon as anyone starts probing, their position shows up false right from the start.'

The Sergeant didn't understand too much of this talk but he understood the lassie who opened the door of Tony's flat. Here, as he afterwards said to the Inspector, he knew he was on home ground. She was tall with long straight blonde hair.

'What is it?' she asked sharply.

'We are police officers. We should like to speak to Mr Flood.'

There was no immediate response. Her eyes gave them careful appraisal.

'He's not in.'

'Oh, but surely,' Moss said without rancour, 'his car is parked outside.'

Her eyelids flickered, and she glanced from one to the other. Her gaze finally rested on O'Keeffe.

'He's not here,' she said. But she did not shut the door.

'We'll wait,' said Moss. There was a little uncertainty about whether the door was going to close or not and O'Keeffe grasped it in a firm hand and held it open for the Inspector. The girl retreated.

As the two men padded across the thickly carpeted lounge, she said again: 'I don't know when he'll be back.'

She flung herself into the depths of a velvet-covered armchair, and then lit a cigarette. Moss sat down, followed by the Sergeant.

It was a large room. The rough-surfaced walls were the colour of stone

160

and the carpet was pale leaf-green. Biscuit-coloured velvet chairs and a corner suite completed the decor. There was in addition a stereo unit and a miniature bar. Two doors led into other rooms. Both were shut.

They waited. The minutes ticked by. The girl finally stubbed out her cigarette, in an ash-tray the Inspector noted, of a rather lovely green glass.

'You're wasting your time,' she said. 'I told you . . . '

'OK, we heard. Right,' said Moss, 'you'll do. Just answer a few of our questions, and we'll be off.'

'What *is* this?' the girl sat up sharply. 'I've nothing to do with Tony's affairs.'

'Don't you believe it,' muttered the Sergeant under his breath.

'Listen,' she said, her voice rising, 'he's out. I don't know when he'll be back. And I'm not answering any questions. Got it?'

'I am quite sure the Inspector has rather *got* the wrong impression,' a lazy voice drawled.

Behind the girl, one of the doors had opened. Tony crossed the room and dropped casually into a vacant chair.

'My secretary,' he gave a nod to the blonde girl, 'has instructions to deny me — but not to the police of course.' He gave a rueful smile and patted the girl's hand, her nails digging into the chair reminiscent of Pompon clutching at Miss Duff's skirt. 'Make some coffee, will you?' he said. 'Don't hurry.'

Without a word, she got up and left the room.

'My sincere apologies, gentlemen,' Tony continued. 'I had no idea. What can I do for you?'

Moss settled more comfortably into his chair. He took out his pipe, carefully filled it, depressed the tobacco in the bowl and after a few false starts finally got it lighting. Pungent smoke filled the room.

'We are investigating this affair of Mrs Nevin's attacker,' he said, between puffs. 'It is possible we may have caught up with the man.'

'I am delighted to hear it,' Tony replied warmly. 'Did you come here just to tell me that?'

The Inspector shook his head. 'By no

means. When we have identified the man, then we shall know where we stand. In the meantime, we are making certain enquiries about the late Andrew Nevin, and you may be able to help us.'

'Andrew!' Tony's voice was sharp. 'What about Andrew?'

'He died two years ago, I believe.'

'Well, what of it?'

'He was quite a young man.'

Tony rose up out of his chair. No languor was apparent now. 'Look here, I don't know what story you've got hold of, but his death was perfectly natural. He died of thrombosis. One of these days, it may be me. We all eat too much, they tell us, and all the wrong foods,' his glance took in the Inspector's comfortable waistline. Moss did not smile.

'Andrew Nevin was a thin man.'

'Look, the whole thing was gone into at the inquest. There was an inquest, you know. You can read about it if you want to.'

'We have,' said Moss quietly. 'But of even more interest to us are the provisions made by the late Mr Nevin in regard to his business. We found that document of very great interest indeed, particularly the section dealing with your position in the event of Mrs Nevin's subsequent decease.'

Tony seemed to have lost some of his colour, but he burst out at once: 'You suspect *me*? The police must be mad! Why, I run that business for her. Without me, there wouldn't be any business. And it's only a twopence-ha'penny little thing anyway. Believe me, any time she wants to buy me out, she's welcome. I have better . . . ' here the gentleman came to an abrupt halt.

He went to the door and opened it. 'Get out,' he said. 'Next time you want to speak to me, you talk to my solicitor.'

Moss rose from his chair, the pipe still in full smoke. 'And who is your solicitor?'

Somewhat taken aback, Tony named the man.

'That will do nicely,' Moss said, as he and the Sergeant made their exit.

13

Vincent Molesworth stood at the end of a long queue. Around him were other queues, equally long and depressing. It was a Thursday morning and the Labour Exchange was crowded. At the other side of the long room, behind their iron grille, public servants worked hard to keep the queues moving. Forms were rubber-stamped and pay dockets issued. And, last of all these lines of men, another group queued for the end product: the week's unemployment money. Bored and still half-asleep, Vincent absent-mindedly read and re-read the notices about penalties for false claims; job creation schemes; industrial training. This was his last week here, pro tem. On Tuesday, rehearsals were due to begin for a Christmas production in which Mr Molesworth had been fortunate enough to secure a part.

The long line shuffled forward. A porter at the door was in conversation with a woman who held a small child. Two boys and an old man sat on a long wooden bench next to the wall. The burly man in front of him was telling his neighbour about some job he had got. He was filling in a buff card, and laughing.

Presently it was Vincent's turn. 'Starting work next week?' said the clerk. 'Sign here. Name and address of employer.' A card was produced and stamped. The clerk wrote busily on the front of a well-worn file. Various documents were bundled into the file, which was then dumped in a basket. Vincent's pay docket was stamped and endorsed. 'Next!' called the clerk.

The actor had progressed to within ten of the pay-out cubicle, when he was hailed by a member of his own profession.

'Vincent! How are things?'

'Not too bad, considering. I'm in the usual Christmas show; probably till the end of January.'

'What's this one called?'

'To tell the truth, I'm not quite sure. It's something about moon men — I've forgotten the title exactly,' and Mr Molesworth looked suitably vague.

His colleague raised an eyebrow. 'Not a name part, by any chance?'

Vincent waved a deprecatory hand. 'I'm one of the astronauts,' he said.

'Too thrilling for you!' responded the friend. 'I've begun work in a little thing myself — revue, you know.' He smiled kindly. 'I'll let you know the date. You must come.' He paused, and then as Vincent began to speak, cut in almost at once: 'Of course you *can't*, can you. I mean — the moon men! Although we might do a little lunch-time thing . . . '

'Quiet please!' said the clerk who was counting steadily.

Vincent's friend threw a look of intense resentment at the figure behind the grille, muttered something under his breath and ended up loudly: 'I wouldn't stay in this place any longer than I could help, anyway!' and took himself off.

Ten minutes later Vincent having collected his money was leaving by the main exit when a woman's hand plucked at his coat. He turned round.

'Hello Kathleen — looking for Paddy?'

The woman's normally impassive face showed signs of anxiety and she said at once: 'Yes — have you seen him?'

'Not this morning, no. I sometimes do on a Thursday. However, there is such a crowd inside today, it would be difficult to recognize anyone! Perhaps he hasn't turned up yet. Did you want him urgently?' and Vincent gazed kindly at the questioner.

Kathleen Tracey, her plain rather lank short hair falling over her face and her tweed coat swinging open, seemed rather unlike her usual quiet self.

She said: 'Did you see him yesterday?'

'Paddy? No I don't think I did. What's up?'

'I don't know.' She twisted her hands together. 'I wish I knew what to do.'

'Well, look here, let's get away from the door — it's rather public and we're impeding the traffic — come over to the side here. Tell me, are you really anxious about him?'

The woman looked up at him. 'Sometimes he is . . . away . . . for a day or so. He doesn't always tell me. I thought I might see him here. He'd be sure to be at the Labour.'

Vincent smiled. 'That's sensible thinking. Have you been here long?'

'Since nine. I saw you go in. I'll wait until one o'clock.'

'Yes, but look here, if we ask them they should be able to say whether he's been here or not.'

'I have his insurance number . . . '

'Wait a minute, I'll go back in and enquire. I'll tell them you're his wife and that you're worried he hasn't shown up. You stay here and keep watch in case he arrives.'

'Thanks very much.' Kathleen pulled her coat around her and stuck her hands into the pockets. 'You probably think I'm daft to be so upset, but I have this awful feeling. I can't shake it off. I keep thinking something must have happened.'

'Wait here,' repeated Vincent, 'and I'll see what I can do.'

'Enquiries' were not unsympathetic when he told his story. They did indeed receive such requests for information, but he would understand that it was not possible to deal with such cases over the counter. Mrs Tracey's best course would be to go to the police. Did she have his social insurance number? Yes. Well, the police had the facilities. They could quite easily check for her. And then there were the hospitals, of course.

On this sombre note, Mr Molesworth reluctantly came away.

'I'm afraid it's no go,' he murmured apologetically to the waiting Kathleen. 'They say the police are the best people.'

She was startled out of her usual calm. 'The police!'

'You needn't mind if it turns out to be a false alarm. They are quite used to that.' He was sorry for the woman. No doubt the police were more familiar with Paddy than she'd like to admit.

'Listen,' he said, 'there's Simms's cousin, what's the fellow's name — Coen, isn't it. He seems like a pleasant sort of chap. Maybe if we had a quiet word with Leo, he could ask his cousin to make a few enquiries. After all, Leo knows Paddy well. He wouldn't want anything to happen to him.'

Vincent's six foot two gazed down on Kathleen Tracey. Her eyes had a half-frozen look.

'You're terribly good,' she said. 'I'm sorry to be such trouble, only I'm half out of my mind.' She caught her breath. 'What'll we do?'

'See if we can get Leo at his yard,' Vincent replied quickly, fearing she was going to break down. 'If he's not there, we'll come back and try the house. Maybe Paddy will have turned up by that time,' he added in what he hoped were comforting tones. And if, subconsciously, he was already playing the role of Captain Intrepid (of the moon men drama) then it had to be admitted he was tall and handsome and looked the part. In real life, he was an easy-going fellow and didn't mind putting himself out to do a favour.

Kathleen said: 'I don't know Mr Simms' business place. Is it far? Perhaps we ought to take the bus.'

A taxi slowly cruised past, and Captain

171

Intrepid immediately stepped out and hailed it.

'This is not the time for small economies,' he said firmly, as he ushered in a protesting Kathleen.

14

Like a good many all-purpose rooms of its type, designed to accommodate differing traditions and activities (none to anyone's real satisfaction) the school hall was not a place in which the artistic spirit might feel at home. To begin with, during the school day sliding partitions divided it into three rooms, of which the end one containing the stage was used for singing lessons. A hardened and embittered piano stood in one corner, and two of the soloists were engaged in moving it to a more central position. The third, a young girl, was collecting chairs and setting out the music-stands.

'You're not thinking of sticking to the original programme, surely?' the 'cellist was expostulating, as he lifted a recalcitrant castor over a knot in the wooden floor.

'Why not?'

The 'cellist straightened his back, and

gave the piano a final push. Then he came round from behind it and lowered his voice.

'She's quite a competent pianist, but her experience is limited,' he murmured, 'so you don't want to put her under pressure. She and I have already been through the Bach twice. That's going to be all right, *I think*. She said she'd put in a little more work on it tonight.'

'Splendid,' said Ruairi, 'so what are you worrying about?'

'You know perfectly well,' the 'cellist whispered back. 'The Brahms, my dear fellow, is *out*. Look, you go ahead with the Mozart sonata. No problems there. Then let her do a piano solo.'

'You mean,' Ruairi put in furiously, 'having been advertised as a Trio, we are going to give the public duos and solos only.'

'Anything is better than giving them a ghastly performance of the Brahms,' countered the 'cellist, whose name was Dermot.

'And whose fault is that,' shouted Ruairi. The pianist looked towards the

174

two men, alarmed.

Dermot caught her glance, and smiled reassuringly. 'Don't mind him, Joan, he's always like this before a concert. Or at any other time,' he added under his breath.

Joan laughed nervously. 'I hope I don't let you two down,' she said awkwardly. 'I can't fill Elizabeth's place, I know. I suppose there's no chance she might be fit to play tomorrow?'

'None whatever,' replied Ruairi in final tones.

The pianist let out a small sigh and seemed to nerve herself to go over to the piano. She sat down, and arranged the music, looking uncertainly towards Ruairi who had turned his back to her.

'Shall we begin with the Mozart?' she enquired, after a pause.

'Good idea,' encouraged the 'cellist. Ruairi still said nothing.

'I said . . . ' she began again, and Ruairi turned around.

'What? Oh yes, the Mozart. Fine — let's start then.'

★ ★ ★

Frances and Janet were returning from a shopping expedition. The streets were already hung with coloured lights, and as they crossed the intersection, a giant Christmas tree stood in their path. Hordes of other shoppers milled around them, intent on making last-minute purchases before the stores closed.

'I sure am grateful,' the American girl was saying, as she clasped Frances by the arm so as to avoid being separated from her in the crush. 'I just did not know *what* I should get Denise, and I did so want her to have something she'd really like. She's been that kind, taking care of all my baggage while I shall be away. And I'm real sad to have to leave, now. We have all been such friends.'

'Tomorrow you'll be in Paris!' Frances was unable to keep the note of envy from her voice.

'Why no — not until Saturday,' responded Janet. 'I shall be travelling by ship, you know.'

'Oh yes, I had forgotten,' and Frances lapsed into silence.

'Do you think anything more will

happen — at the house, I mean?' she asked at length, while they waited in a queue for a taxi.

Janet shook her head. Her dark curls were covered by a little woolly cap with a bobbin on top.

'I surely hope not,' she said.

★ ★ ★

The two cousins met in Organ Place. Leo had parked his handcart at the entrance to the shop and was engaged in carefully dislodging several items piled on the top, when Moss and Sergeant O'Keeffe pulled up in a Garda car. The Inspector got out at once and Sergeant O'Keeffe had the opportunity to observe the resemblance between the two men.

Both were stockily built, Moss being the taller of the two. Leo's complexion was pale-olive in colour and his eyes hazel, while Moss was the possessor of that skin which is apt to look frostbitten in winter. The Inspector's eyes were a remarkable shade of blue, but rather hidden under the dark lashes and very bushy eyebrows. But consanguinity was apparent in the set of the two pairs of shoulders and the slight incline forward of the square-shaped heads.

Leo was saying quietly: 'One of the tenants here is in a little trouble. Do you think you might do something to help?'

'What is it?'

They were mounting the stairs together and Leo turned around to glance at Sergeant O'Keeffe who was following in their wake. The significance of this movement was not lost on the Inspector.

'Which of them is it?' he asked in a low voice.

'It's Mrs Tracey.'

Moss looked a question and his relative hurried on: 'You remember the Traceys who live in the room next to mine.'

Moss's brow cleared. 'Oh yes. Kathleen I think you said her name was.'

'Quite correct. She is anxious to have a quiet word with you about a matter which is troubling her.'

'Of course,' Moss said readily. 'We just dropped in to have a quick word with

Mrs Nevin. Tell your friend I'll see her in a few minutes.'

'I will ask her to come down,' Leo replied gravely, as he continued mounting the stairs.

Denise Nevin greeted the Inspector and his colleague with a watery smile.

'As you can see, I'm very much better,' she said.

They had been admitted by Constance Duff who had risen from her seat by the fire. Opposite to her and comfortably settled in a large armchair, the patient was watching television. She was about to switch it off when the Inspector intervened.

'We shall be only a short while, Mrs Nevin,' he said. 'We have here several photographs of a man and we'd like you to take a look at them and see if you recognize him.'

Denise sat up very straight in her chair, and stretched out her hand for the envelope which the Sergeant proffered to her.

'Take your time,' Moss said, as she spread the prints on her knees and held one out under the light. Almost immediately, she looked up at him, her facial expression a mixture of understanding and fear. Then she took up each of the photographs in turn and examined each carefully.

'Tell me,' she said at length, 'what is it you want to ask me about this man?'

The Inspector regarded her narrowly. 'Why,' he said, surprised, 'naturally we should like you to tell us if this is the man who attacked you the other day, or if there is any resemblance to the man who attacked you.'

'I see,' she replied, and looked at the prints again.

'Well?' he asked impatiently.

'Inspector, this man is dead, isn't he?'

'Yes.'

'How did he die?'

Again Moss turned to her impatiently. 'That need not concern you now. If you recognize him, please say so.'

Constance, who had been endeavouring to give the impression she was watching the television programme, now abandoned all pretence, and spoke directly to Denise: 'What is the difficulty, my dear?'

Before the Inspector could intervene, Denise took one of the prints and handed it to the old lady. Constance peered at the photograph, holding it up almost under her eyes. Then she murmured apologetically: 'I'm afraid my sight is not what it once was. The poor man. He looks as if death did not come easy to him.'

Denise shuddered, and the Inspector curbed his impatience and spoke to her quite gently.

'We do understand what you have been through, Mrs Nevin,' he said, 'and we are only sorry to have to . . . '

He was interrupted by a knock on the door, and he motioned the Sergeant to answer it. Leo stood outside.

'I was not quite sure if you were still here,' he said, while the Sergeant moved back a pace. Leo indicated Kathleen Tracey who stood beside him. 'Please forgive the intrusion. We will wait.'

Moss nodded briefly, and the Sergeant was in the act of closing the door when the two policemen were startled by the movements of Constance and Denise.

Both women had risen. The elder of the two was taking slow but determined steps towards the door, and the younger woman followed her as if in a dream. Constance still held the photograph in her hand, but the other prints had slipped to the floor.

The Sergeant looked to his superior for guidance, but the Inspector gazed blankly at the women, the elder of whom was now between him and the door.

'Please come in,' Constance was saying.

'When I have finished,' Moss interrupted brusquely, but he was halted by the restraining hand of Denise Nevin.

'Please,' she said, 'please — this is terrible. Leo,' she called urgently, in a slightly louder voice, 'did you know?'

He had not known, but he grasped the significance of the photograph held in Constance Duff's oustretched hand. Without a word, he took it from her, shook his head sadly over it, and his other hand closing over Kathleen Tracey's arm in a firm grip, he held out the photograph where she could see it.

The unfortunate woman broke down at once, all her nameless fears realised in that one moment.

'Oh Paddy, *Paddy*,' she sobbed bitterly, crushing the picture between her fingers. 'Paddy, what has become of you?'

15

The story of Patrick Tracey's unhappy demise was not long in spreading to the other tenants, and the whole house rocked under the impact of this news, from *laissez faire* Mr Molesworth in the attic, to voluble Imelda Kelly and Joe Gallagher in the hall flat.

Imelda actually began to consider whether or not she should remove the children, and after a hurried consultation with her father and a series of phone calls to other relatives (to each of whom this horrifying piece of news had of course to be imparted) it was finally agreed that Maeve Kelly, a sensitive eight-year-old, should spend the next few weeks with Joe Gallagher's elder daughter who had a large family of her own.

It was then about eight o'clock, and Joe was not at all anxious to venture out on a cold night to deliver his granddaughter to her aunt living in Ballymun. But Imelda was adamant. Tomorrow, if not actually later that evening, the police would come. The whole house would be turned upside down and questions asked even of the children. She would have sent Donal away if she could, but her sister Pauline had refused to take Donal; in fact, only under pressure had she consented to accept Maeve.

Nor was anxiety about police activity confined to the Kellys. Janet Brown also expressed concern. On arrival, she and Frances had gone straight in to see Denise and so heard the whole story.

'But what do the police think?' Frances asked, bewildered, 'that it was Paddy who . . . who . . . ' She could not bring herself to use the word.

'They believe that almost certainly he was the attacker,' Denise said carefully. She was looking very pale, and her fair wavy hair stood away from her face, haloing her small plump features.

'But *why* . . . ' Frances burst out. 'I mean, how do they know?'

Denise said nothing. Her feelings were not unlike those of Imelda Kelly, and at that moment were echoed also by Janet. The American girl had laid down the parcel she had brought as a leave-taking present.

'It is only a small gift,' she said apologetically, 'for all your kindness to me.'

Denise was touched. 'You shouldn't have done anything like that,' she exclaimed. 'When I think of how good you and Frances have been!'

'It's a shame,' Frances muttered, 'what you went through. But who would have believed it of Paddy? I never thought he had it in him to do violence. A little quiet stealing — that yes. Petty crime. But this . . . I can't get over it. It doesn't seem real.'

Denise did not answer. She was removing the gift wrapping from Janet's parcel. For a little while, she hoped the contents of the package might blot out the memory of the awful photographs. And it was of no use saying it could have been herself, Denise Nevin lying on a slab. Somehow, at the moment, that thought refused to register. And poor tragic Kathleen had actually been taken away to view the reality. Identification was necessary, the police had said.

The parcel proved to contain a beautiful leather handbag, expensively lined and fitted. Denise laughed a little shakily.

'It's quite perfect,' she said smiling as she examined all its inner pockets and unzipped its matching purse.

Janet also smiled. 'I sure do hope you like it. As I said to Frances here, I did not know what to get at all. And I wanted you to have something real special, for all this trip has meant to me.'

The two Irish ladies looked rather embarrassed.

Denise said: 'Shall we see you tomorrow before you go?'

Janet glanced from one to the other, and then spoke abruptly: 'It occurred to me to wonder if I should gct away tonight?'

'Where would you go?' Denise asked.

'I *could* be accommodated at an hotel,' Janet said slowly, 'but it sure seems like running out on you two. It's just that there may be a problem with the police. They will surely want to question all of us.'

'You're right,' Frances said at once. She glanced over at Denise. 'What are the police doing now, do you know?'

'I believe they have the Traceys' room under lock and key until they can examine it. What other precautions they took I don't know. I suppose there's some man on duty floating around in the vicinity.'

'Shall I nip downstairs and see?' questioned Frances. 'If Janet stays here tonight, she may not get away at all tomorrow. What time does your boat leave at?'

'In the late afternoon,' Janet said, 'but the connecting train is due to depart at 13.20. Do you suppose the police may really need my evidence. Perhaps I *should* stay.'

'And what could you tell them?' snorted Frances. 'What can any of us tell them, if it comes to that. But at least we actually *knew* Paddy. How often did you see him, Janet?'

'I don't remember ever seeing him at all!' replied the dark girl with spirit.

'Right,' said Frances, 'come on then. Are you all packed?'

'I am taking only a small travel case and a carry-all,' Janet said, 'but there is my main baggage. I had meant to take it down to the store . . .'

'Leave most of it in your room,' Frances said, 'and give the key to Denise. I'll get the heavy stuff taken down later on. Leo might give me a hand with it.'

Denise nodded. 'That's a good idea. Hurry now,' she said, 'or the Inspector may come back.'

There followed a good deal of rushing about, at the end of which time Frances and Janet met up with Joe and Maeve also setting forth with luggage, and the taxi which dropped Janet at a luxury hotel, carried on out to Ballymun with the other two passengers.

Nor was that the end of arrivals and departures.

Hardly had the running up and down the stairs ceased, and the front door banged, when it opened again quietly to admit Elizabeth Buckley. Her pale anaemic face was almost shrouded by the thick heavy brown hair which hung over her shoulders. She glanced around nervously and quickly mounted the stairs to her own flat. Denise Nevin heard the sounds of movement in the next room, but put it down to police activity.

Still unseen, presently Elizabeth slipped down to the hall and a little later Imelda and Sarah, emerging from the bathroom, met her there. Imelda expressed surprise.

'I didn't know you were back?'

Elizabeth, who had been telephoning, said: 'I've just this minute come in.' Finding the number engaged, she dialled it again.

This time it answered and she depressed the button and said, a little uncertainly: 'Is Ruairi there?'

Imelda waited. Sarah, wrapped in a bath towel, was shivering in the draughty hall. The little girl pulled at her mother's arm: 'Mammy, I'm *cold*.'

Reluctantly, Imelda escorted her youngest into the Gallagher flat. However, in a very few minutes she was back again this time with Donal in tow. She was in time to hear Elizabeth say: 'If he comes in, will you tell him to ring me please. It's very important. Yes. Thank you.'

Elizabeth replaced the receiver, and turned to find Imelda standing behind her. Donal had run upstairs and was now descending by jumping down two steps at a time.

'Donal! Stop that!' his mother cried sharply.

Elizabeth seemed to hesitate. About to mount the stairs as Donal slipped under her outstretched arm, she turned back to the waiting Imelda and said, rather nervously: 'You haven't seen Ruairi I suppose?'

Tact was not Imelda's strong point. 'Since the day of the big row, you mean?' she replied.

Elizabeth flushed, and then said defiantly: 'Since I was here last.'

'Well I haven't seen him myself.' Imelda came closer to the stairs and grabbed hold of Donal. 'Be quiet a minute, can't you?' Turning again to

Elizabeth, she went on: 'He was here you know, one night. There was this terrible commotion overhead. The police were here and took him away.'

'What!'

'Yes, but it was all right,' Imelda added. 'They only wanted to know why he was moving around the house at that hour. I don't know what he told them, but we didn't hear of him being arrested or anything.'

'What happened to him?'

'Nothing, I suppose. He went away with them, that's all. He probably went home to wherever he's living now.' And Imelda's voice held a certain satisfaction. However, it then occurred to her that Elizabeth might be ignorant of the latest dramatic news, and she added in a more friendly tone: 'I wonder you care to come back now, after what's been happening here. I had to send Maeve away, and Janet Brown's cleared out too. You'll have the police questioning *you*, wait till you see.'

Elizabeth, drawing away and beginning to climb the stairs, replied coolly: 'I know all about Mrs Nevin being stabbed. I read of it in the papers.'

'Oh that!' Imelda dismissed the attack on Denise as if it were an everyday occurrence. 'No, I mean this latest thing; about Mr Tracey upstairs. He's dead — stabbed too. And there's some have it, it was him stabbed her.'

'Stabbed who?' Elizabeth cried out, bewildered.

'Denise Nevin, of course.'

'I don't understand. You mean it was . . . what *do* you mean?'

Imelda was only too delighted to explain in great detail, entirely forgetting Donal who disappeared purposefully into the bathroom. The noise of running taps did not worry Mrs Kelly. Her story flowed along, as the watertank emptied and the sounds of its refill grew louder and louder. Elizabeth was a captive audience, her pale face growing ever more frightened and disturbed, until the spell was broken by the phone's shrill clamour. Imelda then turned around to discover that water was gently trickling from under the bathroom door. With a cry of alarm, she abandoned the phone to Elizabeth and rushed to turn off the taps.

Elizabeth picked up the receiver. It was Ruairi.

'I got your message,' he said in a distant voice. 'What do you want?'

The heated exchange between mother and son in the bathroom was perfectly audible in the hall.

'What's going on there?' Ruairi added.

'Oh Ruairi I can't tell you on the phone,' Elizabeth said desperately. 'It's nothing,' she went on incoherently, 'only Mrs Kelly; but something terrible has happened. I only found out about it now. I must have been mad to come back to this place. Everyone is leaving. The police are here . . . '

'The police — *again*?'

'Yes — that's not why I rang though. The concert tomorrow . . . '

'Is cancelled,' he said curtly. 'What *is* going on there?'

'Oh, you didn't cancel? You *knew* I wouldn't fail, no matter what . . . was said.'

'I didn't know anything of the sort,' he

retorted. 'You disappeared into the blue. Dermot was at his wit's end and turned up with this woman, Joan. I soon got rid of *her*. Then he and I had a bit of a dust-up. Nothing really. Anyway, the concert's off.'

'No, why should it be?'

'Will you really play?' he asked suddenly in a totally different voice.

'You know I will. Ruairi, we have twenty-four hours . . . '

'You'd better ring Dermot,' he cut in, adding with unaccustomed humility, 'I rather blew my top and he probably won't speak to me — Elizabeth?'

'Yes?'

'Look . . . about the last time . . . I wanted you to know . . . Oh hell, I can't just like this . . . Ring Dermot then, will you? Where can we have rehearsals? The school hall is closed now. What about the flat?'

'Come round now if you like,' Elizabeth said. Her mood of three minutes ago had evaporated.

'Don't mention about the police — to Dermot, I mean,' warned Ruairi, in something like his usual tones.

Elizabeth was about to protest, when the Department of Posts and Telegraphs indicated that her caller had had his 5p's worth, and the line went dead.

16

The Superintendent had received a very odd report from the Limerick police. This report had passed through many hands before ending up on his desk, and indeed that busy officer found it difficult to understand or believe. For a start, it seemed like the ravings of a lunatic old man. There were points in it which could be checked, of course. No doubt a few enquiries should be made. One of these concerned an address. Obviously that was why the thing had fetched up in his lap — the street mentioned was located in his division. More than that; now that was a curious coincidence, if indeed coincidence it was . . .

These poor loonies, when they read of a sensational case in the papers, they had a way of turning up with the most lurid tales all embroidered on the original version. Probably nothing in it. Still . . . He could imagine Coen's reaction.

He liked Coen. He was a good officer. He worked hard. He got results. But he did his own thing. Sometimes, fortunately, that fitted in quite well with official instructions. Then the case ran on smoothly. The Chief Superintendent was pleased, and praise and thanks filtered downwards. At other times; well, at other times relations were not so happy.

The Superintendent gave it a few minutes thought. He could of course pass it on to one of his sergeants, all in the way of routine. He was actually more than half-inclined to this course of action, when abruptly he changed his mind. The whole thing might well be a nonsense — probably was. However, if by some extraordinary chance it turned out to be the truth, then it was a very serious matter indeed and there was little time to be lost.

He lifted the phone. 'Put me through to Inspector Coen,' he said.

Another person was also giving thought to a forth-coming interview with Moss Coen, although this person's opinion of the Inspector differed greatly from the one held by the Superintendent. To say that Tony Flood had been upset by Coen's visit to the flat was perhaps putting it rather too strongly, but an uneasy conviction was growing within him that he had not really bargained for Coen.

What should he do? Coen might get a warrant to search the flat. Coen had no real evidence. He was sniffing around, hoping for a solution to what had so far been an impenetrable case. No doubt about it, Coen was trying desperately for a break-through. You had only to look at the man to know that if he once caught on to something, there would be no letting go.

Fifteen minutes later, Tony's car drew up outside the premises of Nevin & Flood. Every window in the house showed a light except Frances Loughnane's and the shop itself. Tony got out carefully and quietly walked across to the shop door. His hand already held the keys, and the door opened smoothly. He slipped inside.

He did not put on the light in the shop,

but groped his way forward in the gloom until he came up against the far door. This was not locked and he opened it and stepped through, closing it behind him before putting on the light.

And here his plans met with a slight hitch. He was carrying a parcel. It was not large, but he looked around for an inconspicuous place in which to leave it, and for this purpose chose an empty packing-case which lay on its side next to the wall. Still holding the small parcel, with great care he lifted the edge of the packing-case, finding it heavier than he expected. Something must have been left inside. He put in his hand, and then let out a cry of pain, dropping the case instantly, and only narrowly avoiding dropping the parcel.

An angry ball of fur unrolled itself and hissed at him. Soundly cursing the cat, he took up the now empty cardboard box and lowered his parcel carefully inside. Only when he had finished putting the box away did he pause to suck the blood from his two torn fingers, spitting it out on the floor.

Then he stopped, and listened.

Wasn't that a noise in the shop? A woman's voice and then a man's. What in thunder was Denise doing here at this hour? He'd better put a face on it. Already she must have spotted the car. He opened the storeroom door.

In that second, Pompon sprang out past him, out of the shop and into the street, and Tony Flood found himself confronting Frances and Leo, both toting heavy luggage.

It was Frances who explained matters, and under cover of these explanations Tony pulled himself together. What did it matter now? The thing was done. He was in the clear.

'I just looked in to see everything was all right,' he said pleasantly. With rueful charm, he examined his bloody fingers. 'Didn't see the cat, I'm afraid, until it was too late!'

'You'd better put something on it,' Frances said at once.

'It's all right.'

'No, really, it might turn septic. I have some stuff. I'll get it.'

'Thanks,' he said, smiling at her, and Miss Loughnane whose normal manner tended to be rather straight from the shoulder, smiled sweetly and murmured that she would 'be down again in a minute.'

Leo had meanwhile been stowing away the cases.

Tony said: 'I've finished here whenever you're ready,' and the two men left the shop together, Tony re-locking the front door. 'I suppose I had better look in on my partner,' he added, and Leo said at once:

'I am sure she will be very glad to see you. We have all received a shock here today, and it has been particularly painful for Mrs Nevin.'

'Why, what has happened? Nothing to do with the previous episodes, surely?'

'I am afraid so,' and Leo proceeded to tell Mr Flood all about it.

'The fellow must have been mad!' was Tony's immediate reaction. 'What could he possibly gain by attacking Denise?'

'There is some suggestion that he might have been *paid* to do so.'

'And then silenced when the plan went wrong, eh?' Tony nodded his head and stood for a moment at the entrance to the hallway.

A taxi drew up outside and Joe Gallagher emerged. He mounted the steps somewhat wearily, and the taxi moved off.

'I'm glad that's over,' he said to Leo as he passed in.

'The little one is better away from here,' Leo said gravely 'A good deal of unpleasantness is before us still, I fear.'

In the light of subsequent events, this ominous statement had a prophetic ring.

Frances then appeared rather breathless, her hands full of antiseptic and dressings, and the little knot of men remained while she bound up the damaged fingers. Hearing the conversation in the hall, Imelda came out and joined her father, asking him a few questions in a low tone and receiving monosyllabic replies.

Thus it happened that there were witnesses to the arrival of Ruairi and Dermot — Ruairi first and Dermot about five minutes later.

Four of the party in the hall were so taken aback, they let Ruairi pass in unchallenged. He was carrying his violin-case but no luggage. However, when Dermot appeared they were moved to protest — Imelda first!

Dermot showed no disposition to linger. 'Can't argue about it now,' he said, 'concert's tomorrow, and we're behind as it is. Thought we'd have to cancel, but it *should* be all right now.' He gazed anxiously upwards as he spoke. 'Sorry if we disturb you,' he added perfunctorily, mounting the stairs with the 'cello clasped in his arms, 'but it's only until after the concert.' This last was addressed to them from the landing above.

There then followed the sound of brisk knocking and the door was apparently opened and the 'cellist welcomed in.

'Right cheek, I call it,' Frances muttered, busily rounding off her handi-work. 'After all, the room's not theirs — it's Elizabeth's.'

'But she's back,' piped up Imelda, delighted to be first with the news.

'What!'

'Earlier this evening. And *she* got in touch with the other two. I was here when she rang them.'

Leo said: 'If you will excuse me, I must do a little telephoning myself.'

He waited until he was alone in the hall and then he rang the Inspector.

17

Unaware that the later events of this night were to make Organ Place front page news, the occupants of number 49 went on dealing with such problems as they already had.

The first of these turned out to concern Kathleen Tracey. The Inspector had sent her home, entirely forgetting that her flat had been locked with instructions to admit no one until it had been thoroughly searched. Had Mrs Tracey been a woman of strong will, she might have successfully opposed this decision, at least to the extent of being allowed to take out personal belongings. But Moss Coen was not there, and the Garda on duty, when appealed to, simply stated that the room had been locked by order and would remain so until some other instruction reached him.

The unfortunate woman's resistance was broken anyway. The protective barrier which she had built around the details of her domestic life was now ruthlessly torn down, and her expression was that of a trapped and hunted animal having fought its way back to its own lair only to find the pursuer already in occupation.

In these circumstances, Kathleen Tracey became hysterical.

Doors opened. Leo and Frances appeared first, followed a little hesitantly by Vincent and (from the floor below) Annie Duff. However, when these last two saw what the situation was, both quickly withdrew. The first-floor Trio's oft-repeated bits of Brahms drowned all other sounds in their vicinity, so they were unaware of the disturbance as were Tony and Denise.

When the facts had been elicited, with difficulty, from poor Mrs Tracey, Frances at once turned on the member of the Garda Siochana. Finding him obdurate, she then tackled Leo.

'Surely you could phone your cousin and get this sorted out. Kathleen must sleep *somewhere* tonight.'

Sitting huddled at the top of the stairs,

Kathleen sobbed convulsively.

Mr Simms spread out his hands. 'I would gladly,' he said, 'but I do not know where he may be. When I last spoke to him, he was leaving his office. He said he would call here when he had finished his enquiries elsewhere.' Leo paused and looked towards Kathleen. 'He may arrive quite soon.'

'Well Kathleen can't sit outside her own door until he comes!' Frances burst out.

'No. No indeed. Perhaps if . . . '

'She could have my room,' Frances said at once, 'but there's no bed, since mine is in Denise's flat. I know of course you have that iron bed, but quite frankly . . . '

'Oh no,' Leo said hastily, remembering recent nights of acute discomfort, 'what I was thinking was this — Miss Brown's room is now vacant, and we are in possession of the key.'

Frances looked doubtful. 'Should we, do you think? Harper won't like it.'

'I will undertake to explain matters to Mr Harper, should that become necessary.' Leo moved across the landing and bent down to speak to the woman on the stairs.

Between them they got her into Janet's room. Leo lit the fire, while Frances rounded up spare bedding and some food. Constance Duff came in and sat with Kathleen for a while. When the fire had burned low, she and Frances got the other woman into bed.

Constance said: 'Do you think perhaps a sleeping tablet? The doctor gave me some a little while ago — I don't use them of course — but Kathleen . . . '

'A very good idea,' Frances said.

They stayed with Kathleen until she fell asleep. The time was then about 11.45 p.m.

⋆ ⋆ ⋆

Vincent was having a wonderful dream. All around him were mounds of crisp white snow, light as air, through which he glided along in his red boots. The landscape was monotonous but away in the distance there appeared to be some kind of crater. Small, peculiar-looking animals darted about in the snow. Oh, of course, they were *lemmings*. Funny, he'd never actually seen a lemming, not even a picture of one. So that's what they looked like. Odd sort of sound they made — a high-pitched cry. He stooped down to take a closer look, and then he was falling through space, landing suddenly with a bump. The crying intensified.

He was in his own bed, and there was undoubtedly a cat in the room. What time *was* it anyway? The night was a clear one, and a pale moon shone through Vincent's skylight. He raised himself on one elbow and peered at the battered alarm-clock, which had a luminous dial. One-thirty.

The cat was still crying, but he couldn't make out where it was. His door, he noted, had sprung open. The catch was weak anyway, and he never troubled to lock it. So if the door was open, why was the cat crying? Oh well, let it cry! Pompon, no doubt.

He lay down again and pulled the clothes over his head. The crying ceased. Vincent sighed contentedly and tried to recapture his dream. It had been pleasant, very pleasant. The lemmings were gone now — that was the cat's cry of course ... Oh good grief, here she was! She probably wanted to get into the warm bed. A bony paw, with claws outstretched, plucked the blanket under his chin and a moist nose and whisker tickled his face.

'Go away!' he grunted, and was rewarded by a shrill cry in his ear. This was followed by a thud on the floor and then the sounds of scratching.

'Is there *no* peace to be had in this house,' Vincent grumbled. 'I suppose I'll have to get up. The door *is* open, you know.' This last remark was addressed to Pompon.

But Pompon appeared to want to get out on the roof. When he stood on the floor, he saw that she had climbed up on top of the gas cooker and was making frantic attempts to reach the skylight, pawing at the hasp which hung down over the cooker.

Vincent regarded her in amusement. With her long pear-shaped body, skinny tail and enormous eyes, she was an odd-looking creature.

'I hope you know what you're doing,' he said, lifting the hasp and opening the skylight about a foot.

Without any hesitation, she sprang from the cooker, awkwardly clawing at the edge of the roof, and then disappeared into the night.

'Well, that's one problem less anyway,' he said, closing down the hasp again and securing it tightly. He shivered in the cold night air, and with the back of his hand gave the door a sharp push. The door (as was its wont) banged shut and then sprang open again. Was there to be no end to this? Exasperated, he padded across the room in his bare feet. About to close the door carefully, he hesitated and then peered out. From his vantage point at the top of the house, he commanded a view of the third-floor landing (except Mr Simms' door which was hidden — the back room being a foot or so wider) and also of the well of the stairs. At this hour of night the stairs were unlit, but around the window on the half-landing beneath where he stood, an indeterminate grey area could be seen.

'Is anyone there?' Vincent said loudly.

There was no reply.

Where then was the officer of the law, supposedly guarding the Tracey flat? Vincent descended a few steps. The smell, the origin of his nebulous unease, grew more intense. It might of course be cooking — burnt liver and onions perhaps — such smells being common enough in this house at any hour. He came down to the half-landing and leant over the banister rail. A dense acrid smoke filled his lungs, as full realization dawned.

The house was on fire!

What should he do — go on down? No, anyone left on the top floor might be trapped. Simms — old Simms was there. What about Frances? Wasn't she staying with Mrs Nevin?

Even as these thoughts raced through his head, his long legs were carrying him back up the stairs. He pounded on Leo's door and tried the handle. It was locked. The door of the small front room yielded to his push and he found it empty. He turned back to Leo's, shouting and pounding.

'Wake up, wake up — there's a fire!' he yelled. Would the fellow never hear? Oh, here at last a bolt was being undone. The door was opening.

A rather bewildered Mr Simms emerged in an overcoat and carpet slippers. Vincent dragged him out on to the landing, shouting the unwelcome news as he did so, and even as the smoke now swirled around them.

'But *where* is the fire?' Leo spluttered, by now fully alert. His small nimble feet carried him to the head of the stairs and in a moment he was running down to the half-landing. Vincent would have followed, but the older man waved him back.

'Put some clothes on,' he cried, 'you can do nothing dressed as you are.' For Vincent was clad only in pyjamas.

As the actor turned to obey these instructions, Leo's voice reached him from the next floor. 'And bring towels!' it said.

Constance Duff coughed and wheezed. It was suffocating. After sitting up with Kathleen, she had gone to bed exhausted and, unusual for her, had fallen asleep almost at once. It was the noise which roused her. Odd, because she was accustomed to the noise of people coming and going at all hours. But this was surely different — something was happening, there was an *urgency* . . . She must get up, she must find out. Holy Mother of God, the room was full of smoke. She could not see; she could hardly breathe; her old eyes stung her and tears streamed down her face. She groped for the door.

'Annie! Annie, get up. There's a fire!' However, she appeared to be alone in the room. Annie must have gone outside.

Constance coughed and coughed. She must get her breath, and she must find Annie. Her wool dressing gown hung on the back of the door and she took it down and slowly put it on over the heavy flannelette nightdress. She then felt in the pocket for a handkerchief and having found one she moved across to the washbasin, groped for the tap and turned it on. She soaked the handkerchief in water and held it over her nose and mouth. Someone was coming. She could hear the sounds of voices.

'Miss Duff!' cried a voice from the landing. Through the smoke she dimly perceived Leo.

'I am in here,' she croaked. 'Is Annie with you?'

Leo made his way towards her. 'You must get out at once,' he urged. 'We will find your sister, but you must go now.'

The heat outside was intense, and the floor-boards were hot under the old woman's bare feet.

Vincent had been trying to open the door of the back room. It would not budge.

'What about Denise . . . Frances?' he choked.

There appeared to be some activity on the floor below, but in the dark and smoke it was difficult to know what was happening. A dull red glow covered the stairs, and Vincent asked hoarsely as he battered Kathleen's door: 'Which is it . . . to be . . . stairs or roof?'

Constance had disappeared from view and Leo now emerged from the bathroom on this floor clutching a basin of water and with a wet towel draped on his arm.

'Your hands,' he gasped painfully. 'Be careful of the door. Pressure.' He thrust the wet towel into Vincent's outstretched hands, and the actor stepped back and kicked violently at the door of Kathleen Tracey's room.

Smoke was pouring all around them. Under Vincent's onslaught, the door seemed to sag. Holding the towel to shield himself from the heat, he threw his body against the door and it moved inwards. However, even as it fell, a furnace blast of heat and flames released from underneath the door swept across the landing carrying the door with it, and narrowly missing Vincent as he threw himself to one side. He was then trapped on the lower stairs.

Leo shouted: 'Get back! It's no use.'

In the distance, they could hear Constance moaning: 'Annie — oh, Annie . . . '

Thoughts ran like quicksilver through Vincent's head. He was still clutching the wet towel. He raised a long leg and put one foot on the upper stairs, as he made a spring for the banister above. Catching hold, he pulled himself up and climbed over the top.

Leo had emptied the basin of water on the flames. It was a gesture, no more. 'Leave it — we must get out,' he called, as Vincent hovered on the fringe of the blaze. 'Hurry . . . we must hurry or we shall all be trapped. Miss Duff!' he called abruptly, 'are you there?'

There was a moment of uncertainty. Then:

'Take her,' Leo shouted to Vincent, as she staggered towards them through the smoke.

'I can't leave Annie,' she moaned, 'and Pompon.'

'Don't you worry about Pompon,' muttered Vincent as he dragged Constance past the flames, shielding her head with the towel. A fit of coughing seized him. Was it only ten or fifteen minutes ago that he had opened the hasp of the skylight for the same cat. That simple action seemed to belong to another world entirely.

'She's safe,' he said, hoping to pacify

the old woman, 'she went out on the roof. We'll have to go the same way.'

Was that really on, he wondered? Could a woman of eighty-something crawl through a skylight? And if they did succeed in getting her to safety, what could be done about Annie?

18

Out in the street, several sections of the Dublin Fire Brigade had arrived in response to an urgent summons from Mr Gallagher. He had been awake and had noticed the smoke, but at first paid no attention, and it was not until the door of the back room opened and his grandson had approached with a confiding tug at his arm and a whispered: 'Grampy — there's a terrible red light,' that Joe Gallagher became alert to the possibility of danger. His arrival in the back room coincided with the noise of a window being blown out and, hearing the blast, his daughter woke with a start.

'Dad!' she exclaimed, seeing him over by the window. 'What is it?'

'Get up and get dressed,' he said abruptly. 'Donal, come here. Stay with your mother. Get out as quick as you can. The house is on fire.'

'Oh my God! Where?'

'Basement, I think. Come on.'

Imelda rose up out of the bed so abruptly that Sarah who had been lying awake and regarding her grandfather with wide saucers of eyes, now sensed disaster and began to cry noisily.

Leaving his daughter to deal with the domestic situation, Joe hastily made his way out to the hall and dialled '999'.

'Fire,' he said when the call was answered. There was a pause and then he began to give details. 'It's a four-storey house,' he finished up, 'and there's children and elderly people. Be as quick as you can.'

He clapped down the receiver and went back to the door of his own flat.

'Imelda — hurry up!'

'I'm coming,' his daughter's breathless voice came from inside. 'I'm just bringing a few things. Take the children, will you?'

Joe went in and grasped Donal by the hand. The boy was jumping up and down, shivering with cold and excitement. Joe grabbed up a rug from his own bed and, taking Sarah into his arms, brought the two children outside. He opened the hall door and they went down the steps.

'Imelda!' he shouted urgently.

She appeared in the hall then, clutching various articles. The light in the first-floor front room was on and, although unable to leave the children, Joe who felt he might yet give a warning began to yell 'fire! fire!' at the top of his voice.

One could smell the smoke here but otherwise there was very little evidence of the fire. Must be all at the back, Joe thought. He went on shouting.

Lights came on in the houses around. Curtains were pulled aside, and a face peered out. Joe gestured frantically, although he could scarcely be seen. He shouted again. People began to collect in the street.

Just then, Imelda came running down the steps and Joe gave the children into her care.

'Take them over to the other side of the road,' he directed. 'Wrap yourselves in this rug,' and he put it round her shoulders, 'and whatever you do stay away from the house. No matter what happens, you're not to come back. Stay with the kids. Is that clear?' Before she could reply, he had run back up the steps.

As Joe panted up the first flight of stairs, Ruairi Mitchell, violin clasped in hand, met him on the landing There was a good deal of smoke here, Joe was alarmed to discover, and even as the two men stood together the door of Denise's room opened and a distracted Frances burst out upon them. A hot wave of smoke and grit billowed out behind her.

'Help me with Denise,' she cried. 'I can't rouse her or lift her.'

Ruairi stared at the girl, and coughed as the smoke filled his lungs. He turned back to the front room. Overhead were the sounds of running feet and shouting. This was followed by banging noises.

Elizabeth came out of the front room. 'Is something wrong?' she asked anxiously. The screaming sirens of two fire engines answered her.

'Get out quick,' Ruairi said. 'Tell Dermot.'

'But we can't just leave everything,'

Elizabeth expostulated, 'we must take out what we can — books, music. And what about my piano?'

Ruairi looked at her. For once, there was no anger or irritation in his expression. He caught at a thick strand of her long hair, and tweaked it. 'You're priceless, love,' he said, and kissed her. 'Hey, Dermot, do you want to help carry a piano to safety?' This to the 'cellist who had come out to see what was going on.

'No bloody fear,' responded Dermot, returning to pick up his 'cello. 'Is it really serious?' he asked.

'Looks rather like it. I wonder how they are getting on above?' and Ruairi gazed speculatively at the stairs.

And then it happened. As Joe Gallagher and Frances emerged from the back room with Denise between them, and Ruairi, Dermot and Elizabeth were arguing together on the landing, Denise turned back into the room.

'Andrew's clock,' she said, 'I must take it with me.'

'No, no,' Joe responded, holding on to her.

Elizabeth, who was nearest, said: 'I'll get it!' and brushed past the three at the door. Smoke was everywhere, and she coughed and spluttered.

'Come on quick,' Ruairi urged her, 'this is no time to hang about.' He was already moving towards the stair-head.

Then there was a sudden tearing rending noise accompanied by clouds of smoke and flying sparks.

'The ceiling!' Ruairi cried, 'Elizabeth, you fool, run for it!' Even as he spoke, he ran towards her, breaking through the other four who were confused and got tangled up together.

With a loud explosion, a wall of flame, smoke and debris crashed down from the floor above, the noise almost drowning Elizabeth's screams as she and Ruairi were trapped by the flames.

Dermot, white-faced and inarticulate, stared past the other three, even as the searing heat scorched their faces. Two firemen ran up the stairs behind him, and he turned to them. Joe, however, was the first to speak: 'There's two people trapped in that room,' he shouted, pointing to the inferno.

'If only I'd left the clock alone,' Denise agonized. She seemed to come alive suddenly, where before she held on to Frances and Joe in a kind of stupor. 'The partition!' she cried out to one of the firemen, 'there's only a thin partition between the two rooms.'

Light from the blazing red mass illuminated the stairs. Most of the lights had already fused, and all electricity had now been cut off. More firemen arrived and began to play their hoses on the back room.

'Clear the building immediately,' their chief officer said. 'Come on now — everybody out as fast as you can. We've very little time left.'

Below them, the Gallagher flat was already ablaze although water was now flooding the hall.

'Come on,' he again urged, as the group seemed unable or unwilling to move. 'You can do no good here. Our men will cope. Just leave us to get on with it.' He pointed to the next flight of stairs. 'Is everyone down from the top?'

'There's five or six more up there,' replied Joe, 'unless they got out before.' As he spoke, he and the others were being hustled down the stairs, but at the last moment Dermot broke free and dashed back up and into the front room, where men were already at work on the partition.

Inside the burning room, Ruairi and Elizabeth clung together. He pulled her over to the far wall, in the shelter of the chimney breast. A large wooden press stood there, and he dragged it out and they got in behind it. Neither was hurt much by the falling debris, but Elizabeth's hair was singed and smouldering. Ruairi crushed it between his hands and then rolled up the hair and bundled it under her sweater. The heat was appalling, and the smoke suffocated them.

'Get down on the floor — lie down,' Ruairi urged. He could roughly guess at the position of the door from the noise as fire hoses made the flames hiss and crackle. Smoke shrouded everything. They could not even see the window, where in fact the curtains were on fire.

Down on the floor, with Ruairi half-lying on top of her, Elizabeth gasped for breath.

'Ruairi . . . what chance . . . have we'

'Not much,' he breathed into her hair. His arms came round her shoulders and caught her two hands in his and held them under her body. The heat on his back was so terrible, he thought his spine would melt.

'If you know . . . any prayers . . . say them for both of us,' he gasped painfully, and felt the pressure of her hands in his.

Almost at once they slackened. His head was swimming; he could no longer breathe. Oh God, he didn't want to die. The noise drummed in his ears; the pressure was unbearable. And then oblivion.

19

Moss Coen entered Organ Place in the wake of two more fire engines. When his Superintendent had phoned, Moss had been preparing to leave his office. He listened to what his superior had to say, and promised that something would be done 'in the morning.' Sergeant O'Keeffe could handle this new line of enquiry. The man stationed outside the Tracey flat would go off duty at eleven, and the Inspector would drop by and satisfy himself that all was in order.

He did come, about ten-thirty, and expressed regret over the eviction of Kathleen Tracey. When told that the matter had been dealt with, he was surprised and grateful. The man on duty went home, and after making a few enquiries of Leo, so did Moss.

The news which dragged him out of bed at 2 a.m. came like a blow over the solar plexus therefore. As he drove at high speed through the empty city streets, he cursed himself for a fool. Because of his complacency, innocent lives were now at risk or possibly already forfeited. How could he have imagined the danger was over, at least for the moment? Whatever was at stake in this business, someone had wasted no time. Unless the fire should prove to have started accidentally. But that comforting possibility, he discounted almost at once. Too pat by a long way.

His arrival at Organ Place coincided with the collapse of the ground-floor back room. Nevin & Flood Antiques was now a mass of charred wood and twisted metal. The stairs had already gone, and firemen were using ladders to reach the first floor. The door of number 50 stood open and hoses led up its steps and into the hall. The crowd in the street had grown and was being kept in check by a number of gardai.

Moss identified himself, and was waved through. An ambulance was parked just ahead of him, and another followed him in. Moss approached the fire chief, whom he knew.

'It's a bad business,' this man answered him. The roar of the flames made it difficult to be heard and the two recently arrived fire engines still had sirens going full blast. 'We'll have a job to save number 50 even,' the man bellowed, 'for the wind's blowing the fire this way. Caretaker's been evacuated. House the other side is empty — all offices — and we're doing a holding job there.'

Moss began a long sentence of which the fire officer caught only the word 'casualties?'

'None so far,' he admitted, 'but we have no definite picture of how many people were in the house to begin with. Some got out before we arrived. A Mr Gallagher has been helping us there. His daughter and her children are safe anyway. Mr Gallagher!' he bawled out.

Joe must have been within earshot, because he appeared immediately.

'Tell the Inspector what you've just told us,' the fire chief instructed, hurrying away in response to an urgent appeal from number 50.

'Imelda's OK,' Joe said at once, 'and

she has the two kids with her. They're all right. That was all of us on the ground floor.'

'Two children?' queried Moss suddenly, 'I thought there were three.'

Joe described Maeve's departure in the company of Janet Brown. 'And Mrs Nevin got out unharmed, and Frances Loughnane with her.'

'What about those on the second and third floors?'

'It's hard to say. The stairs were cut off, you see. I think the men are trying to reach them from number 48, or through the roof . . .'

'My cousin Leo — has there been any sign of him, do you know?'

'I heard his voice, once or twice. There was a lot of activity going on up there, just then. That was before the ceiling fell in and trapped the two on the first floor.'

'What do you mean — *trapped*? I thought you said Denise Nevin got out with Frances.'

'Yes, but Miss Buckley had just moved back *in* and the Mitchell fellow and their other friend turned up this evening. Oh, you knew that, did you? Well, there was some concert on tomorrow — tonight I mean — and they were practising. I heard them myself overhead, and they were still at it when the fire began,' and Joe went on to explain what had happened afterwards.

'But Mrs Nevin is safe anyhow?' queried Moss, at the same time watching the first floor window where firemen were at work.

'It was a terrible pity her going back for the clock,' Joe answered him. 'If it hadn't been for that and Elizabeth Buckley trying to get it for her, they'd all have made it down to the street. As it is . . . '

He broke off as two firemen appeared at the window with a bundle wrapped in bankets. It was passed out to men on a ladder and straightway lowered to the ground. Almost immediately, another bundle made its appearance on a stretcher. The men shouted for help for their colleagues inside. As the stretcher was being lowered, another ladder was run up. Three firemen were eventually taken out, two in a dazed condition and one unconscious, and this was followed by the removal of another man. As the onlookers watched, flames and smoke belched from the window and the last two firemen climbed out on the sill and were taken off.

Hardly were they clear, when a warning was issued to all personnel to move back as there was danger of an overhead collapse. Moss looked at the blanket-wrapped victims now being lifted into one of the ambulances. A third person was also receiving medical attention and two men with a stretcher were preparing to move him.

This man was conscious, although dazed, and Moss spoke to him. 'It's Dermot, isn't it?'

'Yes. Do I know you? Sorry, everything's gone a blank.'

'I'm Inspector Coen. I met your two friends at the house,' and Moss looked in the direction of the first ambulance, now pulling away.

'Excuse me, sir, we have to move this man,' a member of the medical team interrupted.

As Dermot was being lifted on to the

stretcher, he stared up at Moss. 'Tell me . . . please . . . they did find them alive, didn't they?'

Moss looked down at the young earnest face, the eyes red-rimmed with smoke. His glance took in the bandaged hands and he remembered this man played the 'cello.

Whoever had been responsible for tonight's *carnage*, he'd get him. For sure.

'They were found alive,' he said.

20

Vincent and Leo, with Constance Duff between them, had made it out to the roof. At one time, the thing looked impossible, for Constance was hardly able to breathe and became more and more inert. Vincent had helped her up to the attic room, while Leo, after a last futile search for Annie, had gone back for some of his possessions and later appeared clutching an attaché case. A man of his bulk naturally experienced difficulty with the skylight, and although his agile legs hopped up on the gas cooker without any bother (Vincent lived in constant fear of an explosion from that source) when it came to squeezing through the small opening, Leo had to make several attempts before he finally succeeded.

The attaché case was passed to him, and Leo then moved into the valley, letting his feet rest on the rising slope of the front roof while his head and arms hung over the skylight. Vincent found a chair and brought it over to the cooker. The cooker was an old one — the property of the gas company — and had a heavy enamelled tray under the burners. This Vincent removed, placing it on top for Constance to kneel on. In this way, with Leo holding her arms and Vincent pushing from the rear, they made some progress. But Constance was a heavy woman, and she was by now completely exhausted.

How they eventually managed it, Vincent scarcely knew. He seemed to be heaving and straining with an unwieldy bulk which at one time seemed in danger of sliding off the cooker altogether (the tray of course was inclined to slide anyway). But Leo held the old arms tightly, and Constance to save herself put forward an extra effort which resulted in her actually standing erect. As Leo dragged her head and shoulders through the opening, she seemed to take new heart. Vincent put all his strength into a desperate shove, and the next thing Leo had slipped back down the roof and

Constance was stuck in the opening, her legs dangling free of the cooker. It was then simply a matter of pushing and pulling, and in another few minutes all three were in the valley, now uncomfortably hot under their feet.

Their original aim had been to make for the skylight of number 50, but after a hasty reconnaissance this plan had to be abandoned, for it was now apparent that fire had spread to the end house. To attempt to gain entry to number 48 meant climbing out of the valley and around the chimney stack.

A hurried conference took place.

'What shall we do?' Leo asked urgently, as the slates grew hotter under their feet. 'At any moment, this roof may go. Let us at least transfer to the roof of the end house. That will gain us a little time.'

Constance Duff lay half-crouched against the slope, her feet bunched under her in the valley. She took no part in the discussion.

'If we once move ourselves over to number 50,' argued Vincent, 'we shall be stuck there and if the firemen don't get to us in time . . . ' he left the sentence unfinished. 'In any case, to take Miss Duff off this roof by way of a ladder — I don't know, it'd hardly be possible, surely?'

'Perhaps,' responded Leo, with an anxious look at the skylight, through which smoke was now pouring in ever-increasing density, 'but the immediate danger is *here* where we now stand. Forward or backward we *must* go.'

Vincent still hesitated. 'Come on,' Leo urged, 'it is too dangerous to delay.'

'Hey, you people down there!' shouted a voice in the background. The two men looked up. Visibility was not good and what light there was, was obscured by smoke. 'Over here, by the chimney,' said the voice again. A beam of light came from that direction and scanned the valley.

The voice turned away. 'There's three of them, sir. Got out through the skylight.'

More men appeared, and two scaled around the chimney and dropped down to the roof. A hose came into play, the stream of water unhappily catching Miss Duff and soaking her.

'Oh!' she gasped, sitting up with a start.

'Get them off that roof!' a new voice directed. Men were helping Constance to her feet. Another man questioned Leo.

'Are you people all from the top floor? What about those on the second floor?'

Leo shook his head. 'We're all there is,' he said.

Two firemen were actually making preparations to get in by the skylight, when an ominous trembling shook the slates under their feet. 'Get them up fast!' came a new call, and Leo and Vincent found themselves hustled forward.

'If only the chimney don't go,' muttered one of the men.

But the chimney, built two hundred years previously, stayed erect.

Vincent managed to scramble to safety more or less unaided. Then Leo was hauled up, clasping his attaché case to his stomach. Finally, Constance Duff, lashed to a stretcher, and dragged along by heaving sweating firemen, reached the comparative security of number 48. They left her on the stretcher while they got her down to ground level.

21

By eight o'clock, a blackened empty shell was all that remained of 49 Organ Place. Fire engines still remained at the scene, for the ruins smouldered and an occasional falling timber sent flying sparks cascading downwards. Number 48 had been saved and the fire brought under control before it could engulf number 50, although the latter had suffered a good deal of damage.

Earlier, firemen had recovered a body thought to be that of a woman. A preliminary examination had been made, but identification had not proved possible as yet.

Of the survivors, Constance Duff was in hospital suffering from shock and exposure. Vincent was at the police station with a weary Sergeant O'Keeffe. Frances had had the bright idea of telephoning Janet at the American girl's hotel. Initial exclamations of dismay and enquiries such as 'but are you sure you are all right?' and 'Denise — she has not been injured, has she?' were immediately followed by instructions to take a taxi to the hotel at once, where, the energetic American was confident, rooms and meals could be provided.

Imelda Kelly had also done some telephoning, in response to which her brother-in-law, Pauline's husband, had turned up in his car, and Mr Gallagher and the Kellys then set out for Ballymun.

Of the other three survivors, Ruairi Mitchell's condition was the most critical. When he and Elizabeth, both unconscious, had been hauled out by rescuing firemen, his clothing was already on fire and his back and legs had received severe burns. Elizabeth's injuries were not as serious, and in her case the main cause of anxiety centred around her respiratory difficulties. Dermot, whose hands and face had received burns, had been kept in hospital also.

All this information was available to Moss on his return to HQ. Kathleen Tracey was dead, of course. The few pitiful charred remains found at the scene were quite possibly hers. But, if so, what had happened to Annie Duff? With Leo's help, Moss tried to piece together the earlier events of the previous evening and, in so doing, Tony Flood's visit came to light.

'He came to see Mrs Nevin, did he?' probed Moss.

'I suppose he did.' Moss's cousin looked extremely weary. His eyelids were puffy and half-closed, and before sitting down he put out a hand to steady himself against the chair. The Inspector's reunion with his relative had been characterized by his usual reticence, and a 'so you made it all right, did you — I'm very glad.'

'Did you speak to Tony Flood?' he pressed on.

Leo planted his two feet squarely on the floor and made an effort to be coherent. He explained about Janet's unwanted luggage and how he had helped Frances to carry it downstairs.

'That was how the second-floor back room happened to be vacant,' he said, with a little touch of bitterness, 'Miss

Brown left us the key, and it was I who suggested we move Kathleen Tracey in there. Frances would have given her own room to the woman. Had it not been for me, Kathleen would now be alive . . . '

Moss interrupted him brutally: 'By what I gathered from Vincent, had it not been for Miss Duff's cat, neither you nor Constance nor possibly Vincent himself would have got out alive. And as for Kathleen, it was I who ordered her room to be locked until it was searched, so if anyone's responsible, I am. Not that I intend to let that worry me. These things happen. It's nobody's *fault*.'

Leo raised his heavy lids, and smiled wryly at his cousin. 'I wish it was as simple as that,' he said, 'but anyhow go on; we were speaking of Tony Flood. While Frances and I were trying to get through the shop with two suitcases and a hold-all — I suppose we made rather a noise — Tony, who was in the storeroom, heard us and came out to see what the disturbance was. He was holding his hand where the cat had scratched him, and Frances said it might turn septic, and went away to get some dressings.'

'Leaving you in the shop with Tony?'

'Yes, that is correct. He remained until I had stowed away the luggage and then he locked the shop and we went up the steps together.'

'Wait a bit; he didn't say *why* he was in the store-room?'

'He simply said he had looked in to see everything was all right.'

'Well, why did the cat scratch him? Did he say why?'

Leo looked at his cousin with raised eyebrows. 'Surely that cannot be important.'

'I wonder,' Moss said. 'I very much wonder.' He pressed a buzzer. 'Get me Sergeant O'Keeffe, will you.'

A few minutes later, the phone rang and he picked it up. 'Yes, Coen here, Sergeant. Do you remember an incident at Nevin & Flood's, the night Mrs Nevin was stabbed: you told me the cat scratched you. How did that happen?'

Moss listened, and a little smile spread across his face. 'OK Sergeant, I get the picture. A *cardboard* box, was it? Right, that's it. Many thanks.'

Moss put the phone down and looked across at his cousin. 'You know, Leo,' he said, 'that cat is at the head and tail of everything in this case,' and he gave a short laugh. Seeing Leo's expression, he went on: 'The Sergeant tells me that after the attempt on Mrs Nevin's life, when he searched the storeroom that same night, he found a number of empty cardboard boxes. In checking these, he discovered one that was heavier than the rest and he put in his hand, with painful results. A cat, presumably the Duffs' Pompon, was curled up in the bottom of the box, and when he disturbed it the cat became alarmed and scratched him.

'Now it seems to me highly probable that our Mr Tony Flood went through the same procedure last night. But the question is, was he casually peering into empty cardboard boxes or did he come there for a particular purpose, a purpose for which . . . '

He broke off, as the phone rang again. 'Coen here,' he answered. 'Oh yes, Sergeant, go ahead. I was coming down anyway, but . . . *What*! Repeat that. Yes. But why was this report not received earlier? They're quite sure? He's made a definite identification? I see. Of course I'm *pleased* — it all ties in. It's just a pity they dragged their heels over it, that's all. We'll have to be quick. OK. I'll join you there. Right.' He put down the phone.

Leo had risen to his feet. 'What is this news?' he asked.

Moss did not answer immediately. He was busy getting another number. When it answered, he said: 'Will you page Mr Williams, please. It's very urgent.'

A pause, and then: 'Hello, Williams? Coen here. Tell me the position as it now stands. Is Frances Loughnane with Mrs Nevin? Oh, she's left, has she. What about Miss Brown, then? She's still there? OK. Now I want you to listen very carefully: it is *vital* that a guard be maintained on Denise Nevin. As soon as Miss Brown checks out, which she will probably do quite shortly — her train departs at 13.20 so I'm told — as soon as she goes, take up your position. Sergeant O'Keeffe and I will be joining you. Our information is that another attack is imminent. So I want no mistake about this: we're up against a criminal who has already killed, and will kill again. There's a great deal at stake here. Right. We're leaving now. That's it.'

He replaced the receiver and grabbed up his coat from a chair. 'You coming?' he asked Leo.

'If I can be of any assistance,' responded Leo, tired but still game. 'I am still waiting to learn your news.'

They went down the corridor together, and Moss said: 'You'd never guess it, but tough, gritty, old Annie Duff has turned up alive!'

Ignoring Leo's exclamations, he went on: 'Not only is she alive — as a matter of fact she had already left the house before the fire started — but she has given us the most astounding information. If what she says is true — and there's no particular reason to doubt her — then this case has taken on a totally new dimension.'

22

In the hotel foyer a number of people sat around, some consuming morning coffee or a mid-morning drink, others waiting for friends before going in search of an early lunch. Those with nothing to do, simply watched arrivals and departures.

Accustomed to the steady comings and goings of well-dressed men and women, these watchers showed unusual interest in an elderly man who pushed through the swing doors and shuffled across to the reception desk. The man was shabby and dirty, and the hotel porter kept him under observation, without appearing to do so. The man spoke to a girl receptionist, who in turn beckoned to a nondescript individual standing by the lift. The onlookers sensed drama.

However, they were to be disappointed. After some moments' conversation, the elderly man was escorted to the lift and disappeared into it. The watchers lost interest.

'Room 404,' Michael Doyle repeated to himself as the lift deposited him in a deeply-carpeted corridor. He looked at the numbers; 451, 452. The room must be in the other direction, at the very end. His mind, unwilling to dwell on the interview ahead, instead harked back to the events of the previous evening.

How curious it had felt stepping into the hallway of Organ Place. He had never parted with the key: surely then he had always *meant* to come back. Anyhow, there he was pushing it into the lock, and experiencing an uprush of feeling as it turned easily. For thirty years he had lived a whole range of different experiences: *he* had changed, but a small insignificant piece of metal still turned the same lock in the same door he had slammed behind him all those years ago.

He was still brooding on the remorselessness of time, when it met him in the face. He had quietly mounted to the first floor, listening to the sounds of violin and piano. Otherwise the house seemed very silent. That was *not* as he remembered it. Full of squalling kids, it had been. He turned a corner and made for the second floor, making room for a woman who was coming down. It was madness to suppose this could be Bernie . . . Could it? The stairs were dimly lit. He peered forward. No, of course it wasn't. On the point of saying 'I wonder could you possibly tell me . . . ' instead the exclamation was wrung from him: 'Annie Duff!'

She did not know him. The gold-rimmed spectacles had slipped down on her nose (the way they always used to, he noticed) and she pushed them back with a firm hand and peered at him, for once at a loss.

'You probably don't remember,' he began, 'but many years ago I used to live here. My wife, Bernadette . . . ' he stopped. He had wanted to say 'Is she alive — does she still live here?' but he could not ask a question like that.

Annie was disbelieving, anyway. 'I don't know who *you* are,' she said sharply, 'but Bernadette Doyle's husband must have died many the long year ago, and indeed she was better off without him, and so my sister and I told her at the time.' This was not strictly true. Constance had not said so.

Michael remembered the sister. A different sort of person altogether. He said: 'That was Constance, wasn't it? And you had a brother living here too.'

'Anyone can reel off names,' Annie snapped, but she was regarding him closely. 'What are you here for now, anyway?'

This was it. He'd have to take the plunge. 'I came to see Bernie,' he answered. 'Does she still live here?'

Annie's suspicions were confirmed. 'She does *not*,' she said at once, 'and if you're so anxious about her, you'd better take yourself off to Dean's Grange! You'll find her there, all right.'

In his bewilderment, he missed the obvious implication, and actually said: 'She lives in Dean's Grange, does she?'

'Oh, she doesn't *live* there. If you were her husband you'd surely know that!'

'You mean . . . when you say Dean's Grange, you mean the cemetery? She's dead, then?' His anxiety mounted. 'When did this happen?' he asked urgently.

'About eight years ago.' Annie's tone was dry.

Eight years! This news had brought him the most tremendous relief, perhaps for more than one reason. All his fears had been groundless then, he thought.

The remainder of the evening's happenings jostled one another in his memory. Annie's hostility had eventually broken down, and in the end she came to admit he might just possibly be speaking the truth about himself. She was also, he perceived, eager to impart information. This she approached indirectly: Constance was looking after a woman, a very sad case — had he perhaps heard about the murder?

To tell him about it, she had brought him up to the flat. Her pleasure at being the possessor of so much news positively *oozed* from her with every gasp of breath. His own feelings were mixed. He had already been to the police: he knew his story took some believing and checking it out was going to cost them. As he listened, depression closed in once more. He was back where he started — worse in fact, because the danger was here at hand and he could see it.

He put it to Annie that her duty was clear. She must come out now, late as it was, and make the identification. That once accomplished, he would know what to do. The powers of persuasion which in years gone by had stood him in good stead at executive board meetings, he now brought into play and she weakened. She hesitated over whether she should tell Constance or not, and finally decided not. Her excuse was that Constance might be upset, and might possibly want to come with her. She would not be gone long.

In the event, they were gone several hours. Once away from Organ Place, Annie entered willingly into his plans and indeed displayed a talent which astonished him. Nothing could have been more natural than her fussy manner as she requested the interview and then, when the person sought appeared, told her little story. While this conversation was in progress, the identification was easily made. When he met her afterwards and revealed it had been a success, she was full of self-congratulation; indeed, positively light-hearted. (Looking forward to telling Constance, and everyone else for years to come, he supposed). His own heart seemed to have moved to somewhere in the region of his navel. But they went on.

At the police station, Annie repeated the whole story with all its ramifications, none of which she omitted. An unfortunate (young) member of the Garda Siochana developed writer's cramp and a search had to be made for a colleague who could type. Only Annie's glance at the clock, and the realization that she had been gone for a number of hours, finally brought this recital to its close.

And then the return to Organ Place revealed the tragedy which had occurred in their absence. Coming on top of her night's excitement, the shock proved too much for Annie and she remained silent and trembling while Michael, even as fearful as she, made his enquiries. When these revealed that Constance was alive and not badly injured, Annie broke down and sobbed with thankfulness, after which Michael had led her away to find her sister at the hospital.

Now, standing outside room 404, Michael glanced around. The door behind him opened and then shut. Someone was approaching from the direction of the lift. He had been here long enough. He would have to go through with it. He knocked. There was no reply. Should he go away? No, they had been very certain at the desk. He knocked again. This time the door opened and a head peered out.

Annie, of course, had explained it all to him the night before, but at the same time he was not prepared for the shock of the resemblance. Bernie, yes, he had expected that. But not Lucy Doyle: the living image of his father's sister, Lucy.

They hadn't told her, of course, and that made it all the harder. To open a conversation by saying 'I'm your father' was clearly impossible. So instead he mumbled something about could he come in?

She looked at him anxiously, puzzled at his shabby appearance. 'You're not . . . not a detective, are you?' she queried.

Should he say yes? Better not. 'I've been in touch with the police,' he managed in a low tone. What *could* he say?

She was letting him in anyway; that was something. The extraordinary thought came to him that Kate would like her. If he ever got out of this mess, he'd try to patch things up with Kate. Maybe they could get properly married this time, and he'd retire to St-Jean-de-Luz which Kate was fond of. And Denise could visit with them, or come and live there if she chose to.

His daydream pleased him so much, he actually forgot for a moment why he was there. At the sound of a light footfall behind him, he turned, hearing a sharp intake of breath and the door closing.

This was it. He had known it would come, but by proxy he had thought. Denise did not understand. She was close to the door, and the other person was advancing into the room, gun in hand.

'Well, Mike,' the cool voice drawled, 'I'll give you credit for making it this far. That dumb fool Whelan kept sending messages he had you under wraps. When I finish here, I won't *need* Whelan and that sure is going to surprise him.

'Denise, honey, I'd be obliged if you'd step a little closer to your parent,' and the voice sang out in triumph.

Denise moved forward as if in a dream. What had been said did not even register. Only the gun. This is not happening to *me*. I shall wake up and none of this will have happened. Even when the gun pointed towards her, she still did not believe.

Only when the police rushed in was the spell broken, and she became aware of the reality of six or seven police officers and the prisoner cursing and screaming as the gun skidded across the floor.

Inspector Coen she recognized. He was panting a little, as with a handkerchief he wiped away the sweat from his forehead before addressing his quarry:

'Janet Doyle, alias Janet Brown, I arrest you for the murders of Patrick Tracey and

Kathleen Tracey and for being concerned in the attempted murder of Denise Nevin, nee Doyle, and for conspiring with others outside the State to attempt to murder Michael Doyle, and I warn you that anything you may say . . . '

The prisoner said plenty but most of it was unintelligible anyway.

23

At the hospital, Annie, by now quite recovered, was pouring out her story to Constance (also much improved) and an admiring circle which included Frances and the rent collector, Mr Harper.

'Who could have imagined that Michael Doyle would return after all these years?' murmured Constance, her head and shoulders comfortably propped up with pillows. Her hand reached out for some of the biscuits being offered round by Frances, and she took one and bit into it thoughtfully. 'And apparently he never even knew Denise existed, so Annie tells me.'

All eyes turned towards Annie, who having extracted a good deal of information from Michael while he was endeavouring to convince her of his *bona fides*, was now in the happy position of being able to tell all.

'He never knew,' she confirmed, 'and it

came as the greatest surprise to him when *I* told him.'

Constance seemed about to make some comment, and then thought better of it. 'But I understand,' she finally said, casting an eye at her sister, 'that Mr Doyle is now a man of very great substance.'

Everyone looked at Annie, and a kind of reverent hush descended.

'When you said you told him about Denise . . . I mean, how did you know?' enquired Frances, at length.

Annie took a deep breath of pure pleasure, but was forestalled by Constance:

'You see we have lived here for so long, my dear. Annie and I and our brother Jack were actually in residence when Michael Doyle and his wife Bernadette came to live in Organ Place.'

'And then Michael left her,' snapped Annie, wanting to get on with the story.

'Oh, not at *once*,' Constance protested. 'No, they were here for a number of years before he left. It was quite sudden. He told her he was going away on business.' Ever fair-minded, Constance added: 'Perhaps that indeed *was* his original intention. He never came back. His wife duly wrote to an address he had given her, but when enquiries were made afterwards it was discovered he had only stayed there for a week or two at most. And the police quite failed to trace him. They decided he had either left the country or was living here under another name.'

'The poor woman was distracted,' Annie put in, unwilling to be silent any longer. 'Up until that time the couple had no family, but shortly after Michael left home Bernadette Doyle discovered that she was in fact going to have a child . . . '

' . . . and so of course,' Constance said, 'she tried to contact her husband at once to tell him this piece of news. Had it not been for that, I believe the matter might have dragged on rather longer. As it was, when she found she couldn't get in touch with him, she became convinced there was something seriously wrong and she went to the police.'

'And what happened then?' asked Mr

Harper. He was waiting to contribute his own bit of information, but it wouldn't bear comparison with this story.

'Well the police did their best of course,' said Annie with a sniff, 'though I'm sure they knew right well he'd just gone off . . .'

'At that time,' Constance added, 'we were still living in the aftermath of the war, and there were certain difficulties in the way of tracing missing persons overseas. Finally, Bernadette came to believe that her husband was dead.'

'And then Denise was born,' said Annie softening, 'such a pretty little child!'

'What I want to know,' Frances demanded, 'is what this has to do with the attacks on her, and Paddy Tracey being killed and all.'

'Well, as to that,' continued Annie, triumphant (for here Constance couldn't compete) 'you see Michael Doyle eventually ended up in America and he went into business there and did very well for himself. And then he met this woman — Kate somebody or other — and went through a form of marriage with her, although Bernadette was of course his *real* wife.

'Anyhow, Michael told me that he and Kate broke up about four years ago when Janet came on the scene. Kate divorced him and he then married Janet. Oh, when I think of that *woman* . . . '

'She was actually his wife?'

'*Legally*, yes,' said Constance with careful distinction, 'because of course you see Bernadette had died a few years previously.'

'But the man wasn't aware of his wife's death?' pursued Mr Harper.

'Oh, no,' Annie responded at once.

'And Janet — did she know?'

'Not then,' the younger Miss Duff went on fluently. 'Michael Doyle told me that Janet and a man called Whelan — they were carrying-on together, you know — actually planned to murder him so that Janet, as his widow, would get all the money. This man Whelan (I hope the New York police, or the FBI or whatever they are, catch up with him) anyway, this man Whelan actually hired men who . . . '

'This happened in New York?' Mr

Harper interrupted.

Annie, knocked out of her stride, paused and regarded the questioner with disfavour. However, she soon gathered momentum again.

'That's right,' she said. 'Well, you see, when Michael found out this dreadful pair intended to do away with him, he let them know he already had a wife in Ireland. He thought this information would upset all their plans, because of course they could not then be sure that Janet was the legal wife. But in fact the pair had already made it their business to find out all about his past life. Anyhow, Janet traced Bernadette to the address in Organ Place . . . '

'Where she also discovered about the existence of Denise, I suppose?' Frances cut in. 'This Kate woman hasn't any children, has she?'

'None,' responded Annie, nodding her head in satisfaction.

'So Denise may well turn out to be an heiress?'

Again Annie nodded, and three of those present expressed their approval.

Only Mr Harper looked unhappy.

'Money can be a terrible curse,' he demurred. 'Here's two people dead and three or four more injured. The house is a shell and the one next door in not too good shape either,' (and all of you homeless, he thought, but he did not say it). At the moment they were just glad to be alive.

Mention of number 50 Organ Place prompted Mr Harper to tell his little bit of news.

'You know about the cat, I suppose?' (He was pretty sure they didn't).

'Pompon!' exclaimed Constance Duff, 'Oh, is the poor thing dead?'

'Far from it,' Harper beamed (his story was going to lose nothing in the telling). 'The caretaker in number 50 went through the rooms after firemen had checked out the building, and he found the managing director's office on the ground floor wasn't much damaged. While he was in there, the man thought he heard a faint cry. Anyhow, he hunted around, and what did he find all warmly curled up together in the managing director's big comfortable chair, only Pompon and a little kitten!'

* * *

Leo of course heard the full story from his cousin. The latter had dropped in to see him at his place of business.

Moss looked tired and sank wearily into one of Leo's broken armchairs. Unsaleable items usually ended up in a corner of the 'office'.

The furniture dealer looked rather wan, and Moss commented on the fact. 'You're not brooding over Kathleen Tracey, are you?'

Leo admitted he was.

Moss regarded his cousin in good-natured exasperation. 'How you and Vincent ever managed to get Constance Duff out through that roof, I'll never know. As for Kathleen, we have heard from Frances that she gave the woman a sleeping pill. All out of kindness.'

Leo shrugged and waved his expressive hands. 'The fire started in that room, I suppose?'

'There and in the basement. I gather from Miss Loughnane that Janet did a certain amount of running around before she left the house 'storing' some of her things in the shop premises. The fire was rigged then, of course. Not that Kathleen Tracey's death was planned. Mrs Nevin was the intended victim all along, and to eliminate *her* that ruthless woman cared nothing for how many other lives were forfeit.'

'And she killed Paddy Tracey also? She took an enormous risk there, surely?'

Moss grimaced. 'My guess is he tried a spot of blackmail and she panicked. Until then, there had been nothing to connect her with the attempts on Denise Nevin's life. She was playing the part of the sympathetic friend to perfection. And the police weren't looking for a *woman*. It was when old man Doyle stepped off his transatlantic freighter and unburdened himself to the Limerick police, it was then . . . '

'But Janet, of course, had no idea that was going to happen?'

'Oh, no. Her boy-friend Whelan sent

word he had Doyle nicely fenced in, and only waited for her nod to go ahead with execution. But Doyle went down so low that Whelan failed to pick him up, and the old man managed to escape. I met him this morning, Doyle I mean. Scarcely recognized him. He's back in business again and the wires are humming. The Commissioner, no less. I'm in high favour at the moment.'

Leo smiled a little. Then a thought struck him. 'Tony Flood was not involved in any way?'

Moss laughed outright. 'You know what that was all about?'

'I should be interested to hear.'

'Well, he came across with it. In the aftermath of the fire, that is. He was so eager to prove he had nothing to do with *that*, he practically begged us to listen. It was about the clock. Not the one in Denise's room, but another which her husband had bought some years ago. She had refused to part with either, in spite of several tempting offers.

'Anyhow, our Tony thought he could do a deal on the side, without her knowing, and he fixed it up through a contact. He had actually taken the clock out to his own flat the day we called, only we gave him such a fright that he brought it straight back! He *says* he had every intention of dividing up the proceeds . . . '

'I wonder,' said Leo, 'I very much wonder.' He became grave.

'Is there any further news of Ruairi Mitchell? Elizabeth is out of danger, so I heard.'

Moss sighed. 'It's hard to know,' he said. 'The doctors are being cautious.' He gave a half-smile. 'But I believe his condition took a definite turn for the better when he found out Joe Gallagher had saved the precious violin!'

THE END

We do hope that you have enjoyed reading this large print book.

Did you know that all of our titles are available for purchase?

We publish a wide range of high quality large print books including:
Romances, Mysteries, Classics
General Fiction
Non Fiction and Westerns

Special interest titles available in large print are:
The Little Oxford Dictionary
Music Book, Song Book
Hymn Book, Service Book

Also available from us courtesy of Oxford University Press:
Young Readers' Dictionary
(large print edition)
Young Readers' Thesaurus
(large print edition)

For further information or a free brochure, please contact us at:
Ulverscroft Large Print Books Ltd.,
The Green, Bradgate Road, Anstey,
Leicester, LE7 7FU, England.
Tel: (00 44) **0116 236 4325**
Fax: (00 44) **0116 234 0205**

Other titles in the
Linford Mystery Library:

A TIME FOR MURDER

John Glasby

Carlos Galecci, a top man in orga-
nized crime, has been murdered
— and the manner of his death is
extraordinary . . . He'd last been seen
the previous night, entering his private
vault, to which only he knew the
combination. When he fails to emerge
by the next morning, his staff have
the metal door cut open — to discover
Galecci dead with a knife in his back.
Private detective Johnny Merak is
hired to find the murderer and
discover how the impossible crime was
committed — but is soon under threat
of death himself . . .

CRYPTIC CLUE

Peter Conway

Fiona Graham, a physiotherapist, is found naked and lying face down in the swimming pool of Croxley Hall health farm where she worked. The coroner's verdict: accidental death by drowning. However, both her father and Golding, the forensic pathologist, disagree with his ruling. Inspector Roger Newton arrives with his assistant, Jane Warwick, to investigate a murder. But when Jane disappears, it's a race to unravel the 'Cryptic Clue' to her whereabouts — and the reason for Fiona's death.

THE BLACK CANDLE

Evelyn Harris

With Chatton Eastwood's history of
Satan worship, the locals believed that
black magic was again rife. And
witchcraft became a cover for premeditated murder. Children, playing
in a quarry, found the body later
identified as Amos White, missing
since the theft of two priceless
tapestries. But the real Amos was
secretly buried in Drearden's Wood.
His killer knew it — so did the
blackmailer — as well as some
inconvenient facts about a lot of
people . . . And death could not fail to
come again.